PROLOGUE

Oxfordshire, England
December 1814

THE BLUSTERY WINTER winds whipped at Madame Zeta's thick woolen cloak, pulling at the tattered folds and allowing the bitter cold to reach beneath to the thin cloth of her worn blouse and skirt. The severe English temperatures during the harsher months had ceased to affect her from the day her daughter, Katherina, was ripped from her bosom.

Nothing—not her lack of a home, threadbare blouse, matted hair, nor her worn boots—caused her any pain. She lacked far more essential necessities than mere possessions. Her heart had been stolen from her.

Before, the organ had beat with such vitality she'd feared her chest could not contain her love. Now, it was empty. Barren. Devoid of anything but hatred, loathing, and a determination borne of years of endless searching, relentless longing, and sleepless nights spent dreaming of her revenge.

From her spot atop the crest of the property, she glared down at the entrance to Shrewbury Gardens.

It had once been a place she'd longed to live and raise a family with her husband, Pierce.

Yet, when she'd arrived that dream had been stripped from her as quickly as her name.

After so many years under the guise of *Madame Zeta*, she'd likely not recognize her old name if someone uttered it…not that anyone but Lavinia knew her true identity.

A'laya De Vere, the Countess of Holderness.

Although, since she'd received confirmation that the duke had died, leaving his only son, Pierce as heir apparent, she was now the Duchess of Shrewbury—if she ever wanted to claim such a tarnished title.

She scoffed at the thought.

She'd rather perish than take the name and title of a man she despised. Never would she be known as anything but Madame Zeta.

But what she wouldn't give to be plain Miss A'laya Banesworth, daughter of an impoverished baron from Nottinghamshire, England. Cherished offspring of Eugene and Chloe Banesworth, Lord and Lady Oderton. If she'd listened to her mother's warnings and not fallen under Pierce's treacherous spell, she never would have wed the then-earl, left her family estate, had his child, found herself abandoned, and her babe stolen from her bosom.

Her chest tightened, as it often did when she allowed her thoughts to meander down the path of her final day living as a proper lady at

Shrewbury Gardens.

If she hadn't been such a senseless fool in her youth, Zeta would still possess a heart. She was thankful her mother hadn't lived long enough to see how shortsighted and simple Zeta had turned out to be.

Unfortunately, she didn't have the guile necessary to prevent her world from shattering right before her eyes. Her own mother—living or not—would have been just as helpless where the old Duchess of Shrewbury was concerned.

Zeta had paid a hard price for her folly since the day she had taken to believing Pierce's lies and trusted his mother to care for her and Katherina.

"My child." A hand, light as a feather but as familiar as anything landed on Madame Zeta's shoulder. "Have I failed ye?"

She turned toward Lavinia, the old woman who'd been a mother to her since the day she'd taken Zeta in all those years ago. Starved, broken, and nearly dead, Zeta had wanted nothing more than to die when the Shrewbury coachman dumped her near Lavinia's caravan. However, Lavinia had told Zeta that one day, she'd reunite with her Katherina. Both women had held onto that declaration of fate. For Zeta, it was a deeply buried and sometimes painful hope, while Lavinia declared the fortune was a prophecy destined to come true.

In that moment, with Zeta battered and wrecked both on the inside and out, she'd decided to live…if only to see her daughter's face once more before her days in this world were up.

With each passing year, it was Lavinia who neared her end, not Zeta. And never did they get any closer to finding Katherina.

Unfortunately, she didn't possess a heart, if

she had it would splinter ever more to see the kind old woman's steady decline.

How many times had Zeta insisted they journey to Shrewbury Gardens to see if Katherina had been brought back to her father's family home? How many times had Lavinia joined Zeta on the very crest they now stood upon, overlooking the place Zeta had expected to call home? No, not Zeta. *A'laya* had longed to call Shrewbury Gardens home. But A'laya and her tendency to see the good in everyone was gone.

Forever.

Madame Zeta was wise enough to know that if she ever expected to see her daughter again, *she* needed to find her. And as things had often been for Zeta, nothing came easily or without great effort.

As they stood on the ridge together this last time, Lavinia's fingers tightened on Zeta's shoulder. "I never meant to fail ye, me dear girl."

"You haven't failed me," Zeta mumbled, setting her hand on Lavinia's cold fingers and squeezing gently. "I have failed myself—and Katherina."

"Soon, I will be gone. But your time, and your search, are far from over."

"No—"

Lavinia tsked at her denial. "It is the way of things, the path of life, as ye very well know."

At Lavinia's words, the necklace, the only thing left to Zeta from her old life besides her heartbreak, warmed at her throat.

They'd traveled, the pair of them, all over England and Scotland. In their journeys, they spoke—sometimes huddled in a freezing wagon bundled in hides, one time before a roaring fire in the early evening outside London proper, and more recently on the coast of Dover during a particularly warm spell amid summer—of the day she'd be reunited with Katherina. In none of their musings had Lavinia not been by Zeta's side when *they* located Katherina.

Together. The pair of them. As they had been since the woman had rescued Zeta from the roadside and taken her in with nary a question.

Lavinia's steady stare scanned the expansive green grounds of Shrewbury Gardens, knowing the hellish torment Zeta had endured at the hands of the estate's cruel mistress, though Lavinia was always too compassionate to speak of it aloud. "I still feel, to me very soul, that your Katherina will be returned to ye."

"As do I." Zeta had spent all her adult life gifting fortunes to those who could spare the coin, and to many who couldn't. She'd learned much from Lavinia, including a knack for reading people—their desires, their fears, and their hearts. "I will never stop searching."

"That is good, my child." The slight weight of the woman's hand slipped from Zeta's shoulder, and she felt Lavinia slipping from this world. Each day passed with Zeta knowing it was one less day with Lavinia near.

The shrubbery to their left rustled, and a woman not much older than Zeta appeared.

"Return to camp," Zeta whispered to Lavinia, nodding back down the hill to the wooded area that gave their caravan refuge from onlookers. "Seek warmth. I will return shortly."

Lavinia stared at the woman as she approached but thankfully acquiesced, turning slowly to return to the others.

"My lady?" The new arrival hurried over to Zeta. She dressed in the Shrewbury servants' garb, with her limp, brown hair tied at the nape of her neck. Beads of sweat formed on her forehead despite the late December cold. "My lady, is that you?"

It had been years since Zeta was mistaken for a lady, despite being raised to take her place in the upper crust of London society.

"Lady Holderness?" the servant said, stopping before her, her eyes narrowing on Zeta. She took in Zeta's disheveled appearance, though she must have found something she recognized as her stare settled on Zeta's weather-worn face.

"I have not gone by that name in many years. But, yes, it is me." Zeta glanced around, fearful her husband, the wretched rakehell, would have someone near to detain her—or expel her from Shrewbury land. "Who are you?"

"My lady, I was the one who—"

Memories returned much like a dagger to her soul. "You helped the duchess collect my things before I was thrown from…Shrewbury." She nearly said her "home", but the estate below had no more been her home than the wagon she'd been traveling in for nearly two decades.

Her home had been with her mother—and later, with Katherina.

The woman dipped her head, clearly ashamed. "No, my lady. I, in no way, wanted to help the duchess. But I had no choice. Was never given a choice if I wished to keep my position."

Zeta eyed the woman, knowing she spoke the truth, yet unwilling to allow her actions to be forgiven so easily. "Where is my daughter?"

The servant's stare returned to Zeta's. "I do not know. I am merely a maid at Shrewbury."

"My husband then?"

The woman's cheeks flooded white, despite the chilly winds. "Last time word came to us, he was living on the Continent after a sordid incident in London."

"He has not returned since his father's passing?"

"No, my lady, though rumor implies he might have gone the way of the duke and duchess." Her tone lowered to a whisper before she continued, "May the Lord bless them in their eternal slumber."

Zeta nearly snorted at the maid's mumbled prayer.

"Who cares for the estate in Lord Holderness's absence?" she prodded, not allowing herself to dwell on that morsel of information. "There must be someone, a cousin or distant relative, who has come forward to claim the title and lands."

"No, my lady. Lord Holderness, err the Shrewbury heir, has yet to claim his title. However, no one disputes that he lives. No one who matters, that is," the maid replied. "Our salaries are paid by the steward. Some of the servants have been released from their posts. Only a few, those needed to maintain the Gardens, have remained. I have heard the steward is in contact with a solicitor in London."

"I should like to speak with him, the steward." Zeta nodded to the woman. She was, after all, Pierce's lawful wife. In his absence, perhaps she could… "Take me to him."

The maid shook her head. "I fear you are not welcome at Shrewbury. The duchess made that very clear before she passed, and the servants were reminded of her decree when you visited the duke several years ago. The magistrate is to be summoned if you even so much as set foot on Shrewbury land."

Zeta's shoulders stiffened as cold outrage settled in her gut. She shifted to stare past the maid to the estate below. "Has the magistrate been called then?"

How had she ever believed she could raise her daughter in such a bitter, unwelcome place, where even the servants feared for their future?

Though she desperately wanted to locate her daughter, Zeta could not jeopardize Lavinia and her people. They'd taken her in, fed her, and given her a place to sleep. She would not be responsible for their presence being reported to the magistrate—and whatever would likely, and swiftly, follow for Zeta daring to defy the duchess's final wishes.

"Of course not, my lady." The servant wrung her hands, her widened stare pleading with Zeta to believe her. "My name is Augusta. I have seen you watching but was unable to come and speak with you."

"Why do you wish to speak with me now? What has changed?" Zeta was not foolish enough to take the servant at her word, not after her employer's betrayal. "I have returned to Shrewbury as often as possible, yet no one has ever offered me help."

"The servants…" The maid bit her lip and clenched and unclenched her hands at her sides. "The servants are afraid."

"Of what?" Zeta demanded.

"Not what, my lady. Whom." She glanced over her shoulder and down toward the manor as if fearing she'd been overheard.

With the duchess gone, there only remained one person to fear. *Pierce.* "And you are not frightened of his wrath?"

"I was for many years, but I have never forgotten your daughter…"

"As I have not," Zeta snapped.

"I wish to help you find her."

Zeta was still unconvinced the maid had anything to offer.

"Why *now*? When you never helped before."

"I couldn't interfere before with the duchess present. Now, with the duke and duchess gone, it is different. The servants, all of us, are worried about our positions. If the duke's son does not return to his place, what will happen to the lot of us, and Shrewbury? The steward cannot keep paying the servants as he does, with no lord presiding over the house."

Tension stiffened Zeta's shoulders as she reminded herself that the people of Shrewbury were not her concern. Perhaps, in a time long gone, they were. But not now...not ever. Only the thought of finding Katherina drew Zeta to Shrewbury, not any misguided affection or concern for the estate's servants.

"I can listen around Shrewbury. Mayhap ask after the babe."

Zeta narrowed her eyes on the maid, daring her to toy with her emotions a second longer.

"I am not the only one who remembers you and the child. Others were never loyal to the duke and duchess, though none will openly admit it. I can convince them. Together, we might be able to find her."

Zeta had never been blessed with anything even close to good fortune—if that were even what Augusta was bestowing upon her now and not another falsehood or thin thread of hope that would soon be severed. Her mind told her to disregard the woman and renew her search, yet her heart...her heart pushed her to accept this simple kindness, even if the maid's offer proved fruitless in the end.

"I can send word to you if I hear anything," the woman promised. "It may take time, but I have faith someone will speak on the matter. Someone will know what has become of your daughter."

"Thank you. I will return to Oxfordshire as often as possible," Zeta offered. The only bit of information she'd been able to gain since the duchess had thrown her from Shrewbury was the mention of a Vicar Elliott. The name had proven useless time and time again. In all her travels, Zeta had never found anyone by that name, nor met a single soul who knew of the vicar or his family.

However, hope—no matter how small—would not escape Zeta's grasp.

Long ago, she'd pledged to find Katherina, or die trying.

She was not ready to die, nor had she given up on locating her daughter—not in all the years she'd been searching.

CHAPTER 1

London, England
September 1821

LORD JOSHUA STUART, second son of the Duke of Beaufort, leapt down from his carriage outside his Cheapside office and signaled for his driver to depart. Discarded morning papers and scraps of waste littered the hard-packed street, and two filthy, ragged mutts scavenged for their next meal. The shingle overhead squeaked, and Joshua made a mental note to oil the hinge and polish the tin signage that read simply: *Solicitor*.

The morning was warm, signifying the afternoon would likely prove sweltering in the tiny confines of his office. It was days such as these that Joshua longed to help all those in need at his proper office off Bond Street. However, those less fortunate, the ones who needed to work every waking hour to keep the pantry stocked, the butcher paid, and the tallow burning, hadn't the time nor the funds to journey across town to the solicitor's office Joshua's uncle had opened nearly thirty-five years ago.

Joshua took his key from his pocket and slipped it into the hole, noting not for the first time the resistance when he turned it. With a bit more force, the key turned, and Joshua entered his building. The bell he'd hung overhead rang as the door opened and swung closed behind him.

His assistant, Henry Portstall, was not due in to work for another hour or so. It was Joshua's routine to arrive early, sort through his tasks for the day, and spend a few minutes alone before the day grew hectic.

Unlike his Bond Street office, this small room, and the even smaller back office cluttered with client folders and reference volumes, was his sanctuary away from everything he found distasteful about the lives of his *beau monde* counterparts.

Here in Cheapside, Joshua was known merely as Mr. Joshua Stuart, Solicitor.

He was not the son of a duke, nor a lord above his neighbors and other small shop owners, in Cheapside.

Those who lived within walking distance came to him for contracts, negotiations, and many times, simply for advice. Tenants wronged by a landlord. A shop owner seeking the proper dowry befitting his daughter. Or a young, unwed mother needing information on education for her son. In all matters, Joshua was confident he could help those who sought out his help. And he did.

Joshua relished the days he was free to spend away from Bond Street. These were the people who really needed his help.

Pausing to light the several candles lining the front room, Joshua smiled as he made his way to the back office where he kept his desk. Shelving units lined the walls, holding his pocket watch collection and an assortment of large books dedicated to the study of English law.

His uncle, Lord Michael Stuart, had always droned on and on about the one thing a man could never get back: time. Time to spend with his family. Time to pursue passions and activities he enjoyed. And, most importantly, time for the betterment of others and the world at large.

It was the sole reason Joshua had opened the small office here after his uncle's passing three years prior. He'd visited the area often for business matters, and when the small building had become available for purchase, he'd leapt at the opportunity. Never once had he regretted the decision or the financial investment he'd made.

Along with both offices, his uncle had entrusted him with his priceless watch collection. . Joshua stored most of them at his townhouse, but he kept a few less valuable, yet no less meaningful, pieces in Cheapside to remind him of the path he'd chosen in life.

An existence of servitude to those in need.

Starkly different than the life of luxury and leisure his elder brother, and their father before him, had chosen. Joshua silently chided himself. He gained nothing from dwelling on his family's excessive lifestyle, nor reminding them of those who lived lives so much less fortunate than they did.

The bell chimed above the front door.

"Good morn," Joshua called. "Please, have a seat. I will be with you momentarily."

He picked up the sheet of paper Henry left on his desk each evening and scanned the list of appointments scheduled for the day. Oddly, his first meeting wasn't until just before noon, though Joshua never turned away an unexpected client when time allowed.

Returning to the front, a courier waited patiently inside the door, clutching a familiar envelope.

It was the same as it had been since he'd taken the position with his uncle's office. Every three months, a courier arrived with an envelope to be delivered to Vicar and Mrs. Elliott at their residence in Cheapside. Their home was located above a small schoolroom, a few doors down from the vicar's parish church. It was how Joshua had stumbled across his current office in the first place.

That had been five years ago when he first met Vicar Elliott, his wife, and their daughter, Miss Katherina Elliott—or as the young woman preferred, just *Kate*.

"Missive for you, my lord." The courier handed the envelope to him and disappeared out the door once more, his satchel, heavy with his daily deliveries, slung over his shoulder.

Scrawled on the outside of the missive was:

Miss Katherina Elliott
C/O Lord Joshua Stuart, Solicitor

After Miss Kate's parents had passed away, her father only six months after her mother, the envelopes had come addressed to Kate, the surviving Elliott. He'd always known the parcel held pound notes, but from whom and for what purpose, he did not dare ask. It was not his concern, something his uncle had reminded him of often.

However, it *was* Joshua's responsibility to see the envelope delivered in a timely manner and unopened. And so, when he arranged his new office, Joshua had instructed the courier to deliver the quarterly parcels to Cheapside for a swifter delivery to Miss Kate.

His uncle had been a meticulous recordkeeper, and Joshua suspected if he truly wanted to know who the parcels came from and what their purpose was, he could find out. However, privacy and confidentiality were things born and bred into any man who took his position as a solicitor to heart. Which Joshua certainly had since his days at Oxford, learning the law from many great men who'd taken their oath to serve.

He glanced out the front window and across the street. A tall, light-haired man, finely dressed for Cheapside, loitered outside the cobbler's shop. His attention seemed focused on a stack of papers clutched in his hands as he read, nearly leaning against the building, but straight enough as to not sully his coat.

Two shops down from the man, the door to Miss Kate's schoolroom was open, and two young boys entered for their daily tutelage, a girl carrying a jug of milk not far behind. After her mother had passed away, Kate had taken over teaching the local children, those blessed with the opportunity to attend school instead of working alongside their families. In return, in lieu of tuition, her pupils gave their teacher fresh eggs, milk, bread, and fabric.

Slipping the envelope under his arm, Joshua left his office, locking up behind himself, and started across the street. The stranger did not turn in his direction nor notice the butcher's wife who'd exited her shop to sweep the walk.

Joshua straightened his jacket lapel and checked that his hair was not ruffled with his free hand.

To say that having Miss Kate Elliott close was an added benefit to renting the building in Cheapside was not worth dwelling on. The elusive draw that always had him staring out the front window in hopes of gaining even the tiniest of glimpses of her was beyond his ability—out of his control—and something Joshua could not deny himself.

He'd longed to invite her to join him for a meal or perhaps a carriage ride to Hyde Park. The friendship they maintained was not to that level. More's the pity. They'd been acquainted through his uncle's solicitor's firm for years, and neighbors after he'd rented his office across the street from her schoolroom, but neither had dared to go any further.

A wave. An afternoon chat. Once or twice a shared cup of tea while her students worked, but never more.

That did not stop Joshua from taking every opportunity to speak with Miss Kate. To ask after her day, to offer help with her students, or to simply be near her. Even if that meant visiting the cobbler next door to her schoolroom in the hopes of catching her eye as he walked past and having her invite him inside for a few moments while the children attended to their lessons or read books in silence.

Voices rose from within the schoolroom housed below Miss Kate's small residence she'd once shared with her parents, though it wasn't the laughter or conversation of her pupils.

One most certainly belonged to Miss Kate, but the other was deep, loud, and…*angry*?

It was not the raised, happy voices of children Joshua was used to hearing floating on the breeze or in through his open office windows and door.

Joshua quickened his steps, peering into the darkened schoolroom as his eyes adjusted to the dim interior.

The children who'd entered as he departed his office wiggled past him and headed back outside. The milk from the jug the girl carried sloshed over the top and nearly splashed the leg of Joshua's trousers, but it saturated the front stoop instead.

"Sorry, Mr. Stuart," Sally Ann said, dipping her head.

"No worries, little miss." He chuckled. "They can be washed as easily as the floor. Who is with Miss Kate?"

"Ol' man Cuttlebottom. And he be right miffed, he is."

Joshua glanced around the schoolroom but Miss Kate and Cuttlebottom, the cobbler from next door, had moved out of sight into the back area. The spare space was used as a storeroom of sorts for supplies and other learning necessities.

"What is he upset about?" Joshua knew children, though seemingly unobservant, listened intently when they suspected something was afoot. Joshua had done much the same when he was young, especially when his father and grandmother embarked on one of their loud rows.

"He comes all the time to call and pester Miss Kate," Sally Ann whispered. "And he smells worse than the butcher shop."

True enough. There *was* a slightly pungent aroma in the room.

One of the boys tugged at Joshua's jacket. "He be want'n Miss Kate's schoolroom for hisself. I be have'n half a mind to thump the old bloke somethin' good."

Joshua stared at the children who'd gathered

around him, silently waiting for him to handle the situation. He recognized some of the young ones by name and others only by sight.

"The lot of you wait here." He gave the group a reassuring smile. "I am certain I can settle the matter for Miss Kate and Mr. Cuttlebottom."

Kate had never told Joshua she was having an issue with anyone, let alone the cobbler. And wanting Kate's schoolroom and residence? Bloody hell, Cuttlebottom had been Vicar Elliott's close friend, and his grandchildren had grown up attending this very schoolroom.

Joshua made his way around the rows of tables with their benches pushed in, Cuttlebottom's voice growing noisier and harsher as he neared.

When he stepped into the back room, Miss Kate stood facing him, her hair swept high atop her head in a severe knot with a few stray curls escaping, her hands on her hips. Cuttlebottom shook his fist in her face, and Kate's bluish-grey eyes sizzled with warning as she took a step toward the old man.

"What is going on here?" Joshua demanded, moving between the pair. Cuttlebottom had no other option but to take a step back, his face molten red with fury. "Miss Kate"—he held up the parcel in hopes of defusing whatever had been transpiring between the pair— "I came to deliver this. The children said Mr. Cuttlebottom had come to visit you."

Her hands fell from her hips, and her expression morphed into her familiar, welcoming smile. Only Joshua feared it was a mask she donned to diminish the severity of the situation he'd interrupted. "Thank you, Mr. Stuart. Mr. Cuttlebottom was readying to depart.

He knows I teach class in the mornings."

"Shall I walk you out, Mr. Cuttlebottom?" Joshua offered when the man made no move to leave.

His glare remained focused on Kate as he said, "I know my way out, *Solicitor*." Cuttlebottom spit out the word as if he'd rather have called Joshua a colorful expletive. "But this is by no means over, *girl*."

The cobbler spun around, nearly tripping over his own feet as he rushed from the room in a huff, slamming the door to the schoolroom behind him.

"Thank you," Kate mumbled, busying herself with collecting a stack of primers from the shelf next to her. "Mr. Cuttlebottom can become quite nettled when the occasion strikes him."

"What was he enraged over?" Joshua paused before adding, "if you do not mind my asking."

Kate scurried past him, her arms full, and her gaze fixed on the uneven wood planked floor in front of her. "It is nothing. Truly."

His interest was further piqued by her avoidance of the subject. "It did not seem like nothing."

"He thinks my father should have sold the building to him before he passed away, that is all."

Joshua followed her into the main room as the door opened, and a dozen children flooded in. "And leave you homeless and without means to support yourself?"

"He claims my father promised him the building to expand his shop, but the paperwork wasn't finalized before my father's death."

Confusion must have been evident on Joshua's face because she asked, "What?"

"I handled all your father's legal dealings.

He never spoke of selling the building to Cuttlebottom, or anyone, for that matter." Joshua thought back to his many dealings with the vicar. "He made arrangements for the building and all his holdings to transfer to you, along with a suitable allowance until you wed." Joshua's body heated at the thought of Kate's wedding.

She set the stack of books on the nearest table and called for Sally Ann to pass them out, before turning back to Joshua. "Until I wed." She laughed. "He was always a man of the old world, was he not?"

Joshua chuckled along with Kate, relishing the sound of her light laughter. His laugh was particularly light-hearted because Kate seemed put off by the preposterous thought of herself wedded to someone.

"He always said you were a man to trust, Mr. Stuart." She sobered, patting a young boy on the head as he took the seat closest to her. "He'd say, Joshua—savior, deliverer, salvation—how can a man of God not think highly of a solicitor christened with the name Joshua?"

"I can find no reason to fault your father's logic, Miss Kate," Joshua responded. "Speaking of delivery, as I mentioned, this parcel arrived for you today."

She eyed the envelope as he held it out to her. Her shoulders tensed, and she scrutinized the package before taking it from his grasp. She did the same each time he delivered one—as her mother had before her—and he reminded himself it was not his place to question its contents or sender.

He cleared his throat, pushing his hand through his hair, likely mussing it. "I can speak with Mr. Cuttlebottom and seek a resolution on your behalf."

Kate's dark brows arched high. "A resolution?" she asked. "A resolution implies there is a problem or an issue that needs remedying."

"Seeing the man's anger moments ago would lead me to believe there is an issue at hand."

"Mr. Stuart..." She smiled, but it did not reach her eyes, and her tone turned severe, any hint of their earlier laughter fleeing. "It is a lark Mr. Cuttlebottom and I embark on every fortnight or so. He comes to my schoolroom, full of bluster, and shouts for a few minutes. Eventually, he calms down, says things are not over, and then leaves. He is old, and I dare say it is his way of expressing his feelings for the loss of his friend—my father."

Joshua glanced around the room as the children looked upon them with nervous energy. In no way did he feel the situation between Miss Kate and the cobbler was simply a lark they played, no matter the tale Kate spun to distract him.

"He is a harmless aging man." She set her hand on his arm and squeezed gently. "Soon enough, he will forget it all and cease bothering me. Please, leave the matter alone."

Joshua inclined his head. "If you insist, Miss Kate."

"I do." Moving on from the topic at hand, she turned to address the class. "Children, what have you to say to Mr. Stuart?"

"Good morning, Mr. Stuart," they sang in unison.

The matter with Mr. Cuttlebottom was far from being settled, at least in Joshua's opinion. While he respected Kate's wishes, he did not trust the cobbler. No man had the right to badger or intimidate a woman, especially a fine lady as kind and selfless as Miss Katherina Elliott. Joshua would keep watch over the situation. If things changed—or progressed—he'd step in.

"A fine day to you all," Joshua responded. "I shall leave you to your studies. Please, listen to your teacher and apply yourselves to your learning."

"And mayhap," Kate called her students' attention back to her, "one day, some of you will study law and become a solicitor yourselves."

The children laughed and applauded, opening their primers to begin their lesson.

With one final glance at Kate, Joshua hesitated, uncertain whether or not he should leave the schoolroom with Cuttlebottom only next door. Kate was utterly alone in the world; her parents gone, and with no other family to speak of. He felt a measure of responsibility to see that no harm came to her. She spent every day in the service of others: teaching, counseling, and helping the children of Cheapside. She didn't need Cuttlebottom's threats shadowing her days. Nor did she deserve the cobbler's harassing visits.

It was a simple enough matter to handle. Joshua could pay Cuttlebottom a visit, have a few words, and explain that as Vicar Elliott's solicitor—and now Miss Kate's—the cobbler could, and should, speak with him regarding matters such as the property belonging solely to Miss Kate. He would not discuss the specifics of Cuttlebottom's presence at the schoolroom nor demand he leave the woman be. Therefore, Joshua was not specifically going against Miss Kate's wishes, only notifying the cobbler that Miss Kate retained Joshua as her solicitor in all legal matters.

Joshua had made such calls before, both in person and via letter with his company signature. This was no different.

Kate slipped the envelope into the front of her apron, opened a book, and began reading to her pupils as each and every little face tuned into her every word.

If he stayed any longer, Joshua feared he'd fall in line with them, take a seat, and never leave, content to lose himself in the melodic lilt of Kate's voice as she read her tale.

He shook his head, gave the room at large a small wave, and departed, making his way down the walk to the cobbler's shop instead of crossing the street. He paused at the shop's threshold as the man he'd noticed loitering on the walk near the butcher's shop threw Joshua a quick glance over his shoulder and started off down the street in the direction of Vicar Elliott's parish.

CHAPTER 2

MISS KATHERINA ELLIOTT did her utmost to keep her eyes from straying toward Mr. Stuart as he left the schoolroom. If anyone listened carefully, they'd note her tone was a bit stilted and raised as she read from *Gulliver's Travels*. Thankfully, her pupils were more engaged with the adventure of the story as opposed to what had transpired as they arrived for their morning lessons.

Though the story fell from her lips without hesitation, her nerves were certainly frazzled from Mr. Cuttlebottom's *visit*. His anger was becoming concerning, even though Kate had known the man and his family her entire life. He'd never proven prone to violence or unrest of any kind before. He was upset, and though Kate was unaware of any dealings between him and her father, she could not blame the elderly man for feeling slighted. Over the last year or so, the gentile man who'd called her father friend had been replaced by an angry tyrant who truly believed *she'd* stolen something from him. She prayed nightly that it was only a matter of time before he saw reason, and their association could return to friendlier terms.

The last thing Kate wanted was Mr. Stuart becoming entangled in the situation.

Though her father had implored her to always trust the solicitor and heed his advice, Kate hadn't the spare funds to pay his service fees. Certainly, hiring a solicitor required a sizeable amount of coin. Slipping her hand into the apron tied at her waist, her fingers grazed the envelope he'd delivered to her. It was a few days later than she'd anticipated. Many debts had been incurred over the last several months that she needed to settle: her tab at the mercantile, the butcher, the candlemaker. And she desperately needed the heel on her boots mended but could not bring herself to visit Mr. Cuttlebottom's cobbler shop nor spare the coin to journey to Smithe's shop several streets over.

As well as teaching the children, she often provided them with a hot meal before they returned home since many of their families worked as tirelessly as she did to make their money stretch far enough to keep the hearth burning at night. Sending her pupils home with empty stomachs was not something Kate would allow if she could, in any way, prevent it.

"Miss Kate," a tiny voice interrupted. "Which side of the egg do *you* crack?"

She blinked, silently re-reading the passage she'd finished without realizing it. "The middle, Constance, I crack the middle."

"Well, I think the larger end is far more suitable," Peter, her eldest pupil, declared, his voice already deepened. A boy on the cusp of manhood. "It is what my father would have done."

Kate smiled. "I am certain you are correct, Peter. However, I hold to my position on the matter." She closed the book and set it aside. "Older children, please open your primers to your arithmetic section. Younger children, practice your numbers on your boards."

As they set about their assignments, Kate moved to the front of the room and sank into the rocking chair her father had crafted for her mother. Her fingers traced the etchings on the side of the armrests. She missed her parents with a fierceness that consumed her most nights. The cobbler's ranting and raving did naught but remind her that she was alone, left to find her own way in this hectic, unpredictable world.

If only she'd had a few more years with her parents, mayhap things would have been different. Perhaps if she'd complied with her father's wishes, she'd have found a suitable gentleman and wed. Maybe she should have followed her mother's wishes and sold the building, moved out of London, and settled in a small village where she could grow her own food and mayhap even procure a dairy cow for fresh milk and cheese.

Kate feared it was too late for such maudlin musings. Besides, the children needed her. They counted on her for their education, and Kate would not let them down. Ever.

Mr. Cuttlebottom would not best her in this situation, nor would she allow him to continue ruffling her feathers as her mother was fond of saying.

She glanced around the room, focusing on the stairs at the rear that led to her residence.

Though her parents had said she hadn't been born in Cheapside, Kate had never known any other home. She'd taken her first steps in the residence above. She'd learned to read in this very room. And she'd sought her prayers each day in her father's parish a few doors down the lane.

The building was brimming with memories—both joyous and heartbreaking.

Though her mother and father had wanted something more, something better for her, Kate was content with her place in the world. She knew her role well, and she excelled at teaching.

She *was* a schoolmistress. It mattered naught that her schoolroom did not boast a fancy name or that her pupils did not possess shiny, tailored uniforms. It was hers and hers alone.

Cheapside was her home. This room and the ones above were all she'd ever known.

And she cherished them ever more, knowing her parents had worked their entire lives to give her this place and her position. Never would she need depend on a man for her survival. Never would she need wed a man and hand over what little she had as a dowry.

Kate would continue as she had since taking over the schoolroom from her mother. The mysterious envelopes she received every three months would go to cover the necessities, and everything else would have to wait. Wait for what, Kate was uncertain.

Leaning forward, she picked at the heel of her half boot as it pulled away from the sole. They would not be mended anytime soon. The schoolroom needed heat, the children needed food, and there were always new supplies to purchase. How was she to educate her pupils without books, maps, and primers?

An idea dawned. If she let out the bottom hems of her dresses, the skirts would reach the floor and keep hidden the travesty of her boots. The notion was silly. The children did not notice her threadbare gowns or worn footwear. Why was she so concerned with it?

She glanced toward the window that looked out over the street as a man walked before her schoolroom, briefly glancing in at her before continuing on his way. The stranger moved out of view when Kate focused the office opposite her with its sign that read: *Solicitor*.

Her cheeks flushed with warmth at the familiar shingle swinging gently on its rusted hooks. Kate need not stand below it to know it creaked softly as it moved in the breeze.

How many mornings had she watched Mr. Stuart arrive at his office in his fancy enclosed coach? How many times had she rushed to the window in her bedchamber in hopes of catching a glimpse of the man as he departed at the end of the day? How many days had she been disappointed when he hadn't arrived to work at all?

Far too many to count, Kate feared.

Mr. Joshua Stuart was a properly learned man who had studied law at Oxford.

Kate was merely the daughter of a lowly vicar and a school teacher, educated enough to teach the basics of arithmetic, spelling, and geography, but not sufficiently learned for University.

Despite both of their presences in Cheapside, they were not part of the same world.

Many nights, she wondered where he went at the end of his working days, or where he was when he didn't arrive at his office in the morning.

She sighed, returning her focus to the children and their studies.

Never had she been unsatisfied with her life. Kate had been raised in her father's image—a pious woman who did not covet excessive possessions. Did not dream of places she'd never visit. And she would not tarnish her father's memory by doing so now. She'd been blessed with the necessities, and that was enough for her...far more than most in Cheapside possessed, certainly.

A tug at her elbow drew her attention.

"Miss Kate," Zachariah whispered, leaning in close, his brow furrowed with concern. "Why are you sad?"

"Why ever do you think me sad?" Kate kept her tone low so as not to disrupt the other students.

"My mama sighs just like you whenever she thinks of my papi being gone."

"Your papi will return from sea soon, I am certain of it." Kate attempted to steer the conversation away from her.

"My mama says the same thing, but that doesn't stop her from crying when she thinks I be sleepin'." At only five, Zachariah had experienced more uncertainty and loss than boys thrice his age should. His father had left on a trading ship bound for the West Indies nearly two years earlier, and the vessel—with captain and crew—had not been heard from since. "Don't be sad, Miss Kate."

She fought against the tears welling, threatening to betray her feelings to the boy.

"Seeing you each day keeps the sadness away," Kate replied cheerfully. "How can I be sad when I am surrounded by the brightest, kindest, and most charming children in all of

London?"

Zachariah snickered, dipping his head.

Kate stood, clapping her hands to draw the attention of the entire room as the boy returned to his seat. "Children," she announced, the weight of the envelope in her apron reassuring. "I think we should journey from the schoolroom today."

"Where to?" shouted Sally Ann, always easily excitable. "Please, tell us."

"The museum?" Constance guessed, bobbing in her seat.

"No, Tattersalls," the boys asserted in unison as they enjoyed watching the grooms at work on the horses.

"How about we walk to Albert's Bookshop and select, together, our next book to read?"

The expressions on a few tiny faces fell in disappointment, but still most seemed overjoyed by the idea of departing the classroom even for a short while.

Kate did not often leave the schoolroom with all her pupils in tow, but today it seemed she needed the outing as much as the children.

The bookseller was only a quick walk down the street. On numerous occasions, after the children had left for the day, Kate would travel the short distance and browse the shelves until the owner closed for the night. She did not often have extra coin to buy books for her own reading; however, Mr. Albert allowed her to enjoy the books in the store as long as she did not bend the bindings or wrinkle the pages.

On a normal day, Kate would not so readily decide to spend her spare coin. Yet, they'd soon be finishing *Gulliver's Travels* and would need another book to keep them occupied.

"Collect your coats and hold hands with

your partner." They'd established rules for such outings. Younger pupils were each paired with an older child. They lined up in a double line and were never to let go of their partner's hand until Kate instructed. Everyone did as told and clasped hands as Kate slipped into her cloak and fastened the brass button near her throat. "Is everyone ready?"

The children all smiled, nodding.

She took the key from the hook near the front door and locked up after the final pair had departed the schoolroom. While her father had been a trusting vicar, he'd always taught her to secure the building if she left—or when she retired above stairs. It was all the more important with Kate living alone, not that it was common knowledge that she resided above the schoolroom without a companion or maid.

The group began down the street at a brisk pace, and Kate kept her eyes trained on the lane ahead of her, her shoulders back as they passed Mr. Cuttlebottom's cobbler shop. The man would not intimidate her. He would not cause her to hide within her home or place of business.

Despite her father's lesson on piety, her mother had given her the confidence and strength needed to live in a world she could not control by teaching her that her actions, emotions, and path were solidly within her grasp. She could not control others, but Kate held sway over her reactions.

That was why she never allowed her emotions to take over when the cobbler confronted her.

In her heart, she feared that her father may have spoken of an arrangement to sell her home to the cobbler. But her mind knew that even if he had, there was no written record of the transaction or her father's intent, which meant Kate was safe.

The door to Mr. Cuttlebottom's shop swung open as she walked past behind the rows of children. She flinched, hoping the old man didn't bring his complaints into the street for all to hear. Most of her pupils lived within a few blocks of the schoolroom, and she could not have her neighbors gossiping about her private affairs. Many were hesitant to trust their children with a schoolmistress at all. Kate wanted nothing to jeopardize her pupils' ability to gain as much knowledge as possible before they grew old enough to work.

To Kate's shock, it was Mr. Stuart who departed the cobbler shop, not Mr. Cuttlebottom.

"Good day, Miss Kate," he greeted, tipping his head to her as she passed. "Enjoy your walkabout."

"Lovely to see you again, Mr. Stuart." Kate nodded but did not stop to inquire about his presence at the cobbler's. He, as any person in Cheapside must, had the need to visit the cobbler's shop every now and again. The soft flapping of her boot sole reminded her of this fact.

Instead, she followed the children as they marched on, suppressing the urge to glance over her shoulder to see the solicitor continue across the street to his office. A small part of her wondered if he'd be staring at her if she turned back, his intense, dark eyes locked on her progress.

Kate shook her head and slipped her gloved hands into the pockets of her cloak, denying herself the irrational urge.

Her father had lectured her often on the evils of wayward thinking and daydreaming about people and places the good Lord would never bless the likes of Kate with. No, it was always best to focus on what she *had* been blessed with in her life as opposed to what she longed for.

CHAPTER 3

JOSHUA HAD ALL but taken up residence at his Cheapside office since he'd spoken with Cuttlebottom three days ago. The cobbler had been less than responsive to his well-worded warning that Joshua handled all of the woman's business matters and the man should stay clear of Miss Katherina Elliott and her schoolroom. When the elderly man challenged him as to what might happen if he disregarded the sage advice, Joshua had hastily threatened to have the magistrate summoned. The foolish man had dared him to send for the authorities.

Dared him!

Instead of doing as he threatened, Joshua had retired to his office and searched the entire building for any record of Kate's father's intentions to sell his building to Cuttlebottom. There was none. Not a single document had been written by the vicar or Joshua's uncle about any such transaction. His concern had been so great that Joshua had sent his assistant to look through the old files at his Bond Street office, as well.

Nothing. Not a single slip of paper to corroborate Cuttlebottom's claims.

Yet, he could not go to Kate about the matter since she'd pleaded with him to refrain from speaking with anyone regarding the argument he'd witnessed.

He'd kept watch of the schoolroom from sunup to sundown, and Joshua was pleased to note Cuttlebottom hadn't returned to harass Kate. Perhaps the man knew full well that there was no proof of Vicar Elliott's intentions to sell the building, and he'd simply taken to pestering the woman out of spite. Or, mayhap due to old age and misremembered conversations. Joshua knew firsthand how cantankerous men could become as they aged. He'd seen it with his own father. So much so that Joshua had moved from the family townhouse in Belgrave Square to his far more modest accommodations in Cavendish Square, the home formally belonging to his paternal grandmother.

Henry cleared his throat at Joshua's side, pulling him from his musings. He glanced up to see his assistant prepared to depart for the evening, a satchel over one shoulder, and his eyelids heavy.

"Go home, Henry." Joshua attempted to direct a stern glare at the younger man; however, he was as tired as Henry was. "You need rest and a hearty meal."

Henry shifted from one foot to the other, his hands gripping the strap of his satchel. "Are you certain, my lord? I could remain for another hour or so and help you. There is the Goosestein matter, and…"

Joshua glanced at the spare desk nearest the front window, the one with a clear view of Kate's schoolroom. The surface appeared cluttered with much to do; he hadn't accomplished anything in days—except keeping an eye trained on the buildings across the street.

"No, no," he said, waving his hand. "I was about to leave for the evening, as well."

"Very good, my lord," Henry dipped his head. "I will be in first thing in the morning. Your calendar is in your office. Would you like me to send your coach around when I collect my horse?"

Joshua had patched the roof and hired a groom to care for the stable behind his office. It was large enough to house four horses and his carriage. Since taking over the building a few years prior, he'd also come to possess a half-dozen cats who thrived on the mice that had once overtaken the small stable.

Shaking his head, Joshua busied himself with stacking the folders he'd carried out to the front desk that morning to keep up the appearance of hours spent toiling over documents. "I planned to take my meal at Mr. Porter's Inn down the road before journeying home."

"Very well. Good evening." The bell chimed above the door as Henry departed.

Joshua sighed, comfortable in the quiet solitude of his office. It was far simpler to feign work when no one was keeping a close eye on him. The sun was descending quickly, and the street between him and Miss Kate would soon be cast in deep shadows. No gas lamps lined the streets in Cheapside, and the night could be very unforgiving in its harshness. While Joshua made his living during the daytime hours, pickpockets, thieves, and miscreants thrived as soon as the sun set.

As he watched the two-story clapboard building across the way, a light flickered in the upstairs window, and someone could be seen moving about the top floor. Kate was likely preparing for the night. He wondered what occupied her many hours when she wasn't teaching the children of Cheapside. What books did she read? What meals did she enjoy? What current events drew her notice? Joshua feared that during the evening hours and the days when the children did not attend school, Kate remained alone for hours—days—with no one to keep her company and nobody to banish the loneliness.

Joshua knew better than most how lonely and solitary life could be. Though he had a large family, they had very little in common. And in Cheapside, Kate had nothing in common with her neighbors. At times, he could envision her gowned in silks—or satin—entering a ballroom alongside London's *beau monde*, and he had no doubt she would fit in perfectly. She would do more than fit in. She would capture the hearts and attention of everyone in attendance.

But that life would ruin a woman of Kate's caliber. She was kind, caring, and compassionate—thinking of others far more than she thought of her own needs. The men and some women of the *ton* would mistake her kindness for weakness and strip her of all Joshua saw as good.

Joshua hadn't spoken to Kate since running into her outside the cobbler's shop after she'd specifically requested he not speak with Mr. Cuttlebottom about the matter he'd overheard. In fact, while he'd kept a close watch on her, he'd been actively avoiding her. He had little doubt she would ask about his visit to Cuttlebottom, and Joshua was not prepared to admit he'd gone against her wishes, though indirectly. He did not wish to quibble over semantics, especially when he was well aware he was in the wrong on the issue.

It didn't matter that he'd done it to protect her, to show the old cobbler that while Kate's family may be gone, she was not alone or without someone to look after her.

Yawning, his eyes grew unfocused, and his stomach growled with a fierceness that clawed at his insides.

Perhaps it was he who needed a decent night's sleep and a hot meal.

He'd lied to Henry when he said that he was planning to take his meal at the inn before returning to his Cavendish Square townhouse for the night. The truth was, he'd requested that his coachman collect him later that evening when he was certain the cobbler had closed his shop and had returned to his residence several streets over. He wished to make sure Kate was safely tucked in bed, and the last candle extinguished from her upstairs window.

Only then would Joshua seek his own home for the night for a few hours of rest before returning to his post before the sun was up again.

He wasn't certain how long he'd need to keep up his watch. Days…weeks…years? Whatever it turned out to be, he'd do it. The cobbler would not take advantage of Kate while and if Joshua could prevent it.

Perhaps Kate was correct, and Cuttlebottom's threats were empty.

Joshua rubbed his face, begging his eyes to

focus—at least for another few hours.

The night was falling, and the streets of Cheapside would be abandoned soon enough, businesses closing and families retiring for the night. Leaving the darkness to those who made their way in life by means that were frowned upon during the daylight hours when polite society roamed the streets.

As if hearing Joshua's silent pleas, the cobbler shuffled out of his shop, a bag hoisted over his shoulder as he glanced around before locking his door. It hadn't taken much to discover that Cuttlebottom resided down one of the alleyways farther into Cheapside, past the inn. However, as the elderly man made to depart, he didn't follow the path he'd taken the previous few nights. Instead, he turned toward the schoolroom.

Joshua pushed from his desk and slipped his arm into his jacket, keeping his stare trained on the man as he hobbled down the street. If trouble were brewing, Joshua would be at the ready.

With a sigh of relief, the old man briefly paused before the schoolroom but then kept moving down the street before turning into the alley two buildings down. Perhaps he was making a delivery—it would explain the large bag he'd slung over his shoulder.

He thought for a moment about following, though he let the notion go when his vision blurred, and a dull ached pounded at his temples.

It was Kate—and her well-being—that consumed Joshua.

If the cobbler wanted to walk the deserted streets of London all night, it wasn't Joshua's concern. If the man was fool enough to risk his safety entering the dark alleys, it wasn't Joshua's place to warn him against it.

He'd given the man quite enough warnings for the time being.

He glanced back at the window above the schoolroom. The light was no longer as bright as it had been. Kate had moved from the front of the building to the back. Was she preparing her last meal of the day? In truth, Joshua had never been to Kate's private rooms above, not even when the vicar and his wife were alive. They'd always met at the parish or in the schoolroom when he'd brought their envelope or other paperwork from his uncle.

A dim light appeared in the schoolroom on the ground floor.

Kate must have forgotten something—a book, her shawl, something more intimate?

At first, he'd feared it would prove difficult to maintain a watch on her and keep the cobbler from pestering her again. However, since the day he'd spoken with the elder man and nearly collided with Kate, she hadn't left the schoolroom. Not even once. She hadn't ventured out to the market, and only had two visitors besides her pupils.

The faint light on the ground floor disappeared, and Joshua imagined Kate climbing the rear stairs, her pristine nightshift fluttering around her legs as she ascended, holding her candle aloft to see clearly in the dim stairwell.

He slid his arms from his jacket and dropped it on a chair, pacing the office.

He was being overly drawn to the situation to the point of allowing his responsibilities to be neglected. Though, in all honesty, both of his offices ran with seamless efficiency even when Joshua dedicated his time and thoughts to other matters.

A small part of his mind yelled at him that Kate was part of those responsibilities, and he was wholly justified worrying about her. He'd managed to convince himself it wasn't that Kate could not care for herself—she had done so for many years—but that Cuttlebottom was unpredictable. Therefore, it was the old cobbler whom Joshua didn't—and shouldn't—trust.

It would stand to reason that since the cobbler had closed shop and departed for the night, Joshua had nothing to fear until the man returned on the morrow. Which meant, Joshua had no reason to linger in his office any longer.

He collected his jacket once more and slipped it back on. Though it was late summer, the temperatures could turn frigid quickly.

His driver would be busy in the stables, awaiting Joshua's call to depart. Perhaps Joshua would relish returning to his townhouse early that evening before everyone had retired to their chambers for the night. Dolly would be overjoyed to spend a few hours with him and perhaps share a meal. The older woman had been a godsend since Joshua had taken up permanent residence in Cavendish. While the elderly woman, his grandmother's bosom friend, saw herself as needing to earn her keep in Joshua's home, her very presence had dispelled the emptiness in the townhouse that had reigned following his grandmother's passing.

Since purchasing the building in Cheapside, he'd become accustomed to closing the office in the evenings. On the rare occasion that Henry stayed late, Joshua remained, as well. Henry had been a welcome addition to the office, and he finished enough work that he was equal to three associates. Despite the assistant's accomplishments, Joshua did not expect Henry to work as tirelessly as he had. More to the point, as relentlessly as *Joshua* had up until a few days prior. He was confident Henry hadn't noticed Joshua's distracted air of late.

The candles extinguished, Joshua opened the front door and stepped into the empty street, turning the lock behind him before slipping the key into the hidden pocket of his jacket.

He stared up at Kate's window, hesitating for a final moment before making his way around the building to the stables. No light shone through the thin drapes. All the lights were out in the cobbler shop, as well.

It was time he returned to his townhouse.

Though he spent little time at his residence, it was the closest place to a home he'd ever known—even if he always sensed *something* was missing. His father's garish townhouse and extravagant country estate were nothing but hollow halls filled with luxuries and wastefulness. Joshua could not understand surrounding himself with such expensive things as rugs, paintings, purebred horses, and such when so many in England went without even the bare essentials.

His father and brother hoarded possessions and wealth, while the children who attended Kate's schoolroom were lucky to have more than one meal per day. Joshua preferred an existence of simplicity over profligacy and extravagance. The life of the *ton* made Joshua uncomfortable and, in many ways, useless. His grandmother had held similar ideals, which had bonded them closer than most.

A brisk breeze blew down the street, ruffling his collar and hair. The crisp cold was welcome on his skin. It was only here, in Cheapside, that Joshua had found his place—a new outlook on the future and what was possible. He was able to help people here…those truly in need of his assistance. Unlike his Bond Street office, were his staff toiled day in and day out, drafting agreement after agreement between wealthy, titled lords who'd never know the struggles of inaccessible legal services and education.

A light flickered in the schoolroom across the street, and Joshua wondered if he'd been caught staring up at Kate's rooms. Had she been watching from inside while he stared at her window? Whoever was in the schoolroom must have moved closer to the front door because the light from the candle grew brighter, illuminating the entire downstairs.

Crossing the street, Joshua smiled. Perhaps he'd ask Kate to join him for a meal at the inn— or she'd invite him in for tea as any woman would likely do if they noticed someone they knew watching them from the street. The ironic twist of his musings was not lost on Joshua. What he should do was warn her of the danger inherent in her uncovered front window. He halted outside the door, waiting for the scrape of the key in the lock.

His chest tightened when he glanced toward the front window and saw flames licking up the interior walls of the room, growing in size and intensity from what he'd foolishly mistaken for a single candle only a moment before.

The building…was *on fire*! And the flames were spreading to devour the first-floor schoolroom.

For a brief moment, Joshua froze, his mind and body unable to work together to process the imminent danger before him or think how to proceed.

As the orange flames moved, growing in

intensity, he hurled his shoulder into the door. The resounding crack could be heard over the music coming from the tavern down the road, but the door did not give way. He needed to get in, to warn Kate, to make certain she escaped safely.

What if she'd found her bed already and was wholly unaware of the flames overtaking the ground floor?

He slammed his body against the wooden door again. It flew open, crashing on its hinges, to reveal half of the schoolroom…ablaze. It hadn't spread as far as the stairs. If Joshua hurried, he could make it up and back down before the fire overtook the room.

"Kate!" Lifting his arm, he used his jacket sleeve to cover his mouth from the smoke and ran across the room to the rear stairway, heat blasting his previously chilled face. "Kate! Kate! Are you up there?"

His sleeve muffled his calls, and he could barely hear them over the pounding in his chest.

He followed the thick, black smoke where it traveled up the stairwell.

Taking the steps two at a time, Joshua reached the top landing without incident and took in a deep breath of less smoky air. He needed to find Kate. He hadn't seen her leave; she had to be inside somewhere. Three doors opened off the landing, and he lunged for the one with the room that would face away from the street. Crashing the door open, he found himself in a small kitchen area with a wood stove, a small table with several chairs, and shelving with assorted foodstuffs. But no Kate. The room appeared separate from the destruction spreading below.

As he left the room, the door across the hall

opened to reveal a startled Kate, her dark hair tucked under a nightcap and a single candle clutched in her hand.

Her eyes widened as she took in the smoke trailing up the stairs and into the two open doors.

"Mr. Stuart?" Panic filled the space between them on the landing.

"There is a fire downstairs," he said, pulling his sleeve away from his mouth long enough to speak without his words being muffled. The heat infiltrated the second floor as he spoke, and the space filled with the smoke from below, seeking an exit. "We need to get out. Now."

It took no further prodding as Kate started for the stairs. He took hold of her arm to steady her as her bare feet tangled in her nightshift in her haste.

"We need to keep our wits about us," Joshua shouted. "The fire is spreading quickly. I had to knock down the door."

They reached the bottom stair, and it was as Joshua had feared; the flames had spread toward the doorway. The air from the gaping door fed the raging blaze.

Kate's glare swiveled from one corner of the schoolroom to the other. "There is a door in the storage room that leads outside."

Joshua pulled her close, noting the frigid temperature of her skin despite the growing heat. Covering her mouth with his sleeve, they huddled together and ran for the storage room. He hadn't been in the room more than a couple of times, but he didn't remember there being a door—or even a window large enough for them to fit through.

"Over there!" She pointed toward the far corner, and he spotted a door, blocked by a waist-high shelf stacked with books. "We can move the shelf easily enough. The key"—she coughed as the air thickened—"is in the lock."

His lungs were burning and heavy. It became more difficult to breathe, and the room temperature continued to rise. He sucked in a breath, begging his lungs to expand even as his throat closed. They needed to get out before the building collapsed on top of them. There would be no hope if they became trapped.

Releasing her, Joshua pulled at the stacks of books, scattering them across the floor, moving the shelf away from the door.

Joshua's panic flared brighter than the flames at their back. There was no key in the lock.

Kate dropped to the floor before the door, her fingers clawing at the floorboards.

The seconds ticked by as the rafters above creaked and groaned as the flames overtook them.

Kate pushed back to her feet, her hand held high with something in her grasp—the key.

They were almost free.

A loud boom shook the room, and a large beam fell from the threshold between the schoolroom and the storage room, trapping them inside. Dread inched up Joshua's spine as he turned back to the door—the only thing standing between them and freedom.

Grabbing the key from Kate, Joshua jammed it into the lock and twisted with such force that he worried the key would break in half. Despite it being rusted from disuse, it began to turn before halting.

Suddenly, Kate was at his side, attempting to help with the door.

"The key," he warned. "It's stuck."

"It has to open." She clawed at the door, utter terror distorting her face, her breaths leaving her in short, labored huffs. "We need to get out."

Joshua stared around the darkened room for anything he could use to smash the key loose. He spotted the thick cane the vicar had used in his final years to help him walk the block between the parish and the schoolroom. It leaned against a wall, untouched by the blaze.

With both hands, Joshua moved Kate away and grabbed the cane, holding it over his head before he brought it down. The blow dislodged the metal, and Joshua turned the key, pulling the door open. He could feel the flames eating through the walls at his back, threatening the room in which they stood. Thankfully, the knob did not scorch his palm. Though in his haste, Joshua was not confident he'd have noticed if it had.

Their path was clear, and their freedom stood on the opposite side of the threshold.

Joshua pivoted back toward Kate, but she no longer stood there.

She'd crumpled to the floor in a heap, her nightgown covered in dust and soot. Her breathing was labored, made extra difficult by her exertion in trying to find the key and helping with the lock.

There wasn't time to stop, no time to think—only react.

Joshua lifted Kate into his arms and pushed through the door and into the alleyway that extended in both directions. Smoke followed them outside. Sirens blared in the distance.

An alarm must have been sounded to call the fire brigade.

Joshua hurried down the alley to the narrow

passage that would lead back to the main street and his office, Kate still held tightly to his chest. He needed to summon a physician to make sure she hadn't inhaled too much smoke or had been burnt anywhere.

"My home?" she asked, lifting her head from his chest. Panic and disbelief narrowed her eyes as she attempted to gain sight of her schoolroom.

"The brigade is on the way," Joshua soothed, hurrying down the passageway until he arrived at the main street, in the exact location he'd spotted Cuttlebottom disappear down earlier. A line of men, armed with buckets, had formed in the street leading down to Vicar Elliott's old parish and the closest well for fresh water. Man after man transferred buckets full of water down the line until Joshua spotted his driver and stable hand at the front, attempting to stop the fire.

"Chapman! Chapman!"

His driver turned sharply. When he spied Joshua, he thrust his bucket into another man's hands and hurried over. "M'lord. Ye building was locked up tight. We sent a lad fer the brigade but wasn't certain where ye be."

More men arrived to help put out the fire as Joshua continued cradling Kate. His driver removed his jacket and covered the woman's exposed legs.

"She needs to be seen by a physician," Joshua said. "Have Elmer fetch Dr. Brown and meet us at the townhouse."

"Right, m'lord," Chapman called over the shouting men. "I'll tell Elmer and meet ye at the carriage."

The water engine rumbled down the street, and men set about pumping the water that fed the long hoses with a steady stream of liquid. The streets were filling quickly with onlookers;

the gossip mill already turning as people spied him, clutching Kate to his chest as they watched the fire slowly being extinguished.

"M'lord." Chapman hurried back over. "We need to take Miss Kate away from the smoke."

Her body trembled in his hold as the evening chill soaked through her thin nightgown and the coat his driver had laid over her. The fright had turned her skin clammy, dispelling the warmth from the fire.

Joshua hurried toward the passageway that led to his stables and his waiting carriage.

He deposited Kate on the seat across from him and fumbled to remove his jacket so he could wrap it around her shivering form. Her eyes were closed, but he sensed that she was awake.

"The brigade will have the fire out soon," he whispered, adjusting his driver's coat to cover her bare feet. "Just rest. Deep breaths."

He sat opposite her, watching her chest rise and fall as her breathing slowed. He gently brushed the hair from her face. Her nightcap had been lost somewhere in their haste to free themselves from the building.

He'd been right to be worried about Kate and her safety. Could Cuttlebottom have set the fire? Indeed, he'd been angry, but enough to jeopardize Kate's life?

"Thank you, Joshua," she mumbled, her eyes remaining closed. "My father was correct about you."

"Shhhh," he called, sitting back as the carriage started for Cavendish Square.

"Salvation…"

Joshua nearly chuckled as the immediate sense of danger receded, and they were spirited across London toward his townhouse. "No, I was only in the right place at the right time. Now, rest. I will wake you when we arrive."

Her eyes closed, and her breathing evened out. The smell of smoke hung heavily in the air of the enclosed carriage.

Joshua would let her rest, at least until they arrived at his townhouse, and the physician was ready to attend to her.

He kept watch on her as the carriage swayed gently, noting a dark smudge of soot streaked across her cheek, and the singed fringes of her nightshift. His own jacket was torn at the elbow. The weight of Kate's situation settled in: she was safe and unharmed. However, they'd both been nearly killed, and Kate's home was in ruins. Had the fire been set or merely caused by an unattended candle in the schoolroom? Was Cuttlebottom responsible?

There was plenty of time to discuss the elderly man. For now, Joshua wouldn't bother her with such matters. Tonight, he'd make sure she suffered no lasting effects from the fire. Tomorrow—or the next day—they'd deal with the cobbler and Kate's ruined home.

The carriage rocked rhythmically as it traveled down seemingly endless London streets. A wayward curl fell across Kate's face and caressed her cheek. The interior of the coach was lit by two lanterns on either side, making the bridge of freckles across Kate's nose visible. Her eyes fluttered behind her eyelids, and she sucked in a deep breath on a gasp. The fire was only just extinguished, but the nightmares of the ordeal were already beginning.

CHAPTER 4

KATE ROLLED OVER, heat warming her face as she stretched out her legs, their stiffness nothing new. She'd always slept the most soundly curled into a tight ball. The ache in her legs and back was the same. The hearth that heated the upper floor of her home was not close enough to her room, even if she left the door open, to bring any kind of deep warmth. Neither were her sturdy, woolen blankets soft and inviting. The straw mattress she'd used since her childhood had forever been unforgivingly hard and lumpy.

The hairs at the nape of her neck stood on end.

Something wasn't right.

In fact, something was certainly *very* wrong.

She squeezed her eyes shut, feeling around for the edge of the bed. With arms extended in both directions, Kate could not reach either side. What she did encounter was yards and yards of blankets that were cool and smooth to her touch, not tattered and coarse like the ones on her bed. The quilt her mother had worked diligently on for nearly six months before Kate's eighth birthday was not within her reach either. The cushion under her head felt more like a cloud than her usual straw and horse-hair-stuffed embroidered pillow.

Despite it all, Kate did not have the sense that she was in danger. Quite the contrary, actually. The perceived ease she felt startled her far more than awakening in a strange bed in a room that could not possibly be hers.

She thought hard on the previous night—or had morning not dawned yet? Kate remembered eating a light meal as she hadn't gone to the grocer in nearly a fortnight. Slipping into her nightgown, Kate had twisted her hair into a knot and tucked it under her nightcap to keep her curls from tangling in her sleep, then climbed into her small bed. She'd forgone her nightly reading to yet again conserve her tallow in case a midsummer storm moved in that made it necessary to light candles in the schoolroom for the children.

Nothing had been amiss as she'd willed her mind to stop churning. She'd fallen to sleep.

However, she most certainly was not in *her* bed above the schoolroom any longer.

Even the smells were different. She didn't smell tallow but beeswax. The linens were infused with lavender and, mayhap, scents of a meadow—not that she'd ever been to a true meadow. The fire in the hearth did not reek of the cakes that she bartered for in exchange for Sally Ann's schooling. No, the heat reaching her had the distinct scent of coal.

Kate hadn't been afforded the luxury of

coal—or wood—since shortly after her father had passed away.

She was not in her Cheapside home with the small window in her chambers that afforded her an obstructed glimpse of the London Bridge. Besides the scents and the softness of the bed, the sounds were also foreign to her. Or, better put, the *lack* of noise was unusual.

Opening her eyes, Kate took in the expansive room. The bed was easily the size of her entire chambers in Cheapside. Heavy draperies covered a bank of windows that stretched the length of the wall in front of the bed she rested in. The furniture was dark wood; however, the bedding was a pale blue that diminished the masculinity of the chamber somewhat. To her left, a great hearth with a grate did, indeed, burn coal.

"Good morning." She turned to the right to see Mr. Stuart—Joshua—masked by shadows and lounging in a large chair. He was no longer Mr. Stuart, kindly neighbor and solicitor. He was now Joshua as he'd discarded his coat and his cravat hung loosely around his neck. His sleeves were even rolled to his elbows. "How do you feel? Does your chest ache?"

Kate pushed up to sit, and the blankets that had been pulled high to her chin fell down to pool at her waist. She no longer wore the long nightgown her mother had sewn for her years ago. Instead, the cotton nightdress she wore was made of crisp satin with a row of bows leading from her throat down to her waist and perhaps beyond.

"Where am I?" she gulped, clutching the high collar of the gown as her cheeks heated.

"Do you remember anything from last night?" Joshua leaned forward in his chair, his fingers tightening on the arms of the furniture, but his expression remained hidden in the shadows.

"I—" Kate closed her eyes, and images flooded her mind. Joshua standing on the landing outside her bedchamber door, backlit by flickering light, the smells of smoke and burning wood overwhelming. "There was a fire—in the schoolroom." She paused, remembering the whole of it: the terror, the smoke, the heated flames. "Where am I?"

It seemed far preferable to question him on such mundane, trivial things rather than inquire as to the destruction of the only home she'd ever known. The same building that allowed her to gain a wage to care for herself without assistance.

His head dipped, seemingly knowing what she longed to ask but in some unspoken way understanding that she was not ready to hear it. "After the fire brigade arrived, I brought you to my home and had my family physician see to your injuries."

She frantically moved in the bed, pushing the blankets down until she could inspect her entire body. As the daughter of a pious vicar, Kate knew she should feel embarrassed and uneasy about being alone with Joshua—in *his* home. They'd been unattended on several occasions in the past, but never in such a suggestive and inappropriate way. It seemed all the worse that Kate's eyes settled on the exposed skin at his throat.

"You had no burns and didn't inhale too much smoke." His words soothed her panic. "When the physician left, I had my housekeeper make you more…comfortable. Your nightgown was soiled from ash and soot and smelled of burnt things. I've sent it to the laundress for cleaning."

Housekeeper? Laundress? Family physician?

"I do not understand." She glanced around the lavish room. It was not the home of a modest solicitor from Cheapside. Kate had long known that Joshua was an educated man, but she had assumed he attended University as a servitor and not as an independent member. The room was far too grand for the likes of a gentle commoner. "*Where* are we?"

Joshua was undoubtedly a man of means if not something far more.

"My townhouse in Cavendish Square." He rubbed at his chin and looked past her toward the hearth. "It was the only suitable place I could think to bring you."

"You, Mr. Joshua Stuart, Solicitor, have a home in Cavendish Square?"

He shrugged, his eyes alighting on her, yet Kate sensed a barrier between them that'd never been there before. "It once belonged to my paternal grandmother."

"Yet your office is in Cheapside?" She kept her stare trained on him, attempting to gauge any hint of deception in his answers or tone.

"I prefer to help those in actual need." He sighed, reclining once more in his chair and clasping his hands in his lap. "I do not have much to my name, except this home and my offices."

"*Offices?*" Obviously, their circumstances and personal notions of *not having much* varied greatly.

"The office in Cheapside where I use my time and finances to help the people living nearby, and my building off Bond Street."

Kate had met Joshua in her youth when he'd first completed his time at University and came around to deliver parcels to her father. He'd been fresh from school and had taken a post as his uncle's assistant. They'd had more occasion to become acquainted when he opened his solicitor's office across the street from the schoolroom.

In reality, she didn't know much about him at all.

"Who *are* you?" She breathed the question on an exhale. There were many merchants and shopkeeps who, despite their successful businesses, did not have the means for multiple properties plus living quarters in one of the most coveted areas of London.

When he didn't immediately answer, she feared he hadn't heard her.

Reluctantly, he stood and paced toward the bank of windows and then back before stopping at the foot of the bed. "I am Lord Joshua Stuart, second son of the Duke and Duchess of Beaufort."

"You lied to me. To us *all* in Cheapside?"

"No, no," he said, his shoulders stiffening at her accusation. "I have only withheld my place as a second son. However, I *do* have little to my name and have worked hard at my schooling and career in law—with the backing of my uncle, who is my father's younger brother, also a second son."

"Little to your name?" Kate scoffed, remembering the dreadful pungent aroma of burning dung she'd been forced to heat her home with for the past several years. "You have far more than most, *my lord*."

Her stare turned swiftly to a glare, while he simply turned and returned to his chair, lowering himself as if the weight of the world rested upon him.

The son of a duke, even a second son, could not know the trials and tribulations of those in Cheapside and beyond.

"Did my father know?"

"Know what?"

"That you masqueraded as…as…" The words escaped her at the same time she recognized her anger was misguided. He'd rescued her from a burning building. Risked his own safety. And she had been taught at a young age not to cast stones. There was much about herself that she wondered about. Did that mean she was purposely deceitful? Certainly not. He'd done nothing but help. Many of those he worked with were parents of her pupils, who would have otherwise been unable to afford the services of a solicitor. Much like she, Joshua devoted his life to others. "I'm sorry, I—"

He held up his hand, silencing her. "Your father and my uncle had a long association, spanning over fifteen years. To answer your question, yes, Vicar Elliott knew that my uncle, and in turn I, were of noble birth. He also understood that every man is entitled to make his own way in life and live accordingly."

"You speak as if your beliefs align more naturally with the people of Cheapside than those of your noble brethren." Why would a man in possession of a grand home and a fancy office in the fashionable part of London *choose* to do business in Cheapside? Kate rarely had need to venture outside her neighborhood, and she only encountered nobility on the rare occasions when they sought out the East End for cheaper goods than could be found in other areas of London.

How had she never noted the aristocratic set of Joshua's chin or his cultured speech? Perhaps she preferred *not* to notice, leaving her free to believe they were of a similar class. That despite his education and her lowly birth, they could live in a world where he was simply a handsome, engaging man, and she a woman with the ability to notice. Over the years, she'd watched many of her pupils, and even some she considered friends, meet men of their age, fall in love, and marry. Yet, for some reason, this seemed far from Kate's reach.

And her thinking was not always due to any kind of class difference.

"To that, I would respond with a resounding 'yes'," He shook his head, rubbing his hands down his trousers, coming to rest at his knees, his chin rising defiantly. "I—and my uncle before me—am not a man who lives like most lords. I aspire to a greater purpose, as did my predecessor. Your father—as a man of God—understood us more than most."

"Why did he not tell me?" She would not share with Joshua that there was much her father and mother hadn't shared with her. Information about Kate they'd taken to their graves.

"Likely because he did not see it as important or relevant to our association."

"How can it not be relevant to our *association*?"

Her question hung in the air as a knock sounded at the door. She stared, as did he. She was uncertain what about her held his notice; however, Kate had the sense she was seeing Joshua—*truly* seeing him—for the first time. Not as the son of a duke. No, as he'd said, that was not who he was, only *what* he was. Kate knew far too well the stigma that came with being born to certain parents. He was the second son of a duke, but he was more than that. Just as Kate longed to be more than a vicar's daughter.

Joshua had accomplished his feat.

Kate…had not.

"Enter," he called.

The door opened, and an elderly woman dressed in a simple black frock with a white apron entered the room pushing a tea cart.

"Oh, dearie," she cooed with a welcoming grin. "Just look at you."

Kate could not help but return the woman's smile.

"How are you feeling, dear girl?" She halted the cart on the far side of the bed, blocking Kate's view of Joshua. "Your color has returned, and I must say you certainly look better than when you arrived last evening. Would you not agree, my lord?"

"I most certainly agree, Dolly."

The woman chuckled as she bustled about with the cart. "Sugar or milk, my dear?"

It took Kate a moment to realize the woman—a maid?—spoke to her. "No, thank you."

"No tea?" The woman's brow spiked.

Kate leaned to the side, attempting to gain Joshua's notice, but his stare was focused on the older woman. "Ummm, pardon. I meant, no sugar or milk."

"Ah, well." The woman tsked but she winked at her. "Mayhap you will try some with your next cup."

It was as if she knew Kate could not afford the luxuries of fresh milk and sugar. Had Joshua confided in the maid that Kate came from Cheapside? Her hand went to her hair, knowing how unruly it got if left unattended. Her mother had spent hours in Kate's youth brushing through the knots and plaiting her strands to prevent painful tangles.

"Thank you, Dolly, for bringing tea," Joshua said, still blocked from view by the portly woman. "Miss Kate is likely parched. And mayhap hungry?"

"'Tis my job, my lord." After handing Kate her tea, the maid set about preparing a plate of toast with marmalade. "Now, I shall leave the pair of you. Remember, Joshua, the doctor said she needs rest. And you do, too. You won't do anyone any good if you're exhausted."

Dolly wagged her finger at Joshua before pushing the cart from the room and shutting the door in her wake.

The plate of toast sat next to Kate on the bed as she sipped her tea. The temperature of the brew was perfect and strong, much like her mother had enjoyed.

"Dolly is more my family than a servant," Joshua shared. His stare lingered on her, and he made no move to depart.

"It is not my concern." Kate set her tea on the side table when her stomach growled. Perhaps it hadn't been the best idea to have but a small meal the previous night. "It is said that all proper lords have servants. I cannot imagine the complexities of running a household as large as this without any staff."

"She was my grandmother's companion for twenty years. After her passing, I could not turn the woman out. She had no family besides me." Joshua stood, moving to the bank of windows and pulling the draperies back to reveal the rising sun. "She would not remain here on charity. So, she assumed the role of my housekeeper. Not that I see her as such or ask much of her."

"I can understand a person's need to feel useful and earn their keep." Isn't that what Kate had always attempted to do? Kate bit into her toast, savoring the tangy plum marmalade as she chewed.

With the drapes pulled back, Kate was able to see the room more clearly. An old painting of a woman with long, brown hair hung above the hearth. Behind her stood a man with an upturned chin, piercing green eyes, and a nose that appeared startlingly similar to Joshua's. On the woman's lap sat a babe dressed in vibrant blue hues. Standing near the man was a toddler, another boy. The portrait was striking, yet none of the four in it appeared happy.

"My grandparents," Joshua spoke. He'd returned to the bedside. "With my father and uncle. These were Grandmother's chambers."

Something tightened within Kate at the tone of his voice when he spoke. Longing and a sense of loss permeated the air between them.

"After my grandfather passed and my father took over the dukedom, Grandmother retired here to Cavendish Square at her family's home." His tone softened. "My sibling and I were left to stay with her for weeks, sometimes months at a time. My parents traveled most of the year and did not relish their children as hangers-on. Grandmother was a kind, loving woman. She, with Dolly's help, basically raised my brother and me. I was very close to both women."

"What of your brother?" Kate asked. It was another surprising fact about Joshua that she'd never thought about—he had a brother. Kate sometimes longed for such a connection, a kinship with a sister or brother close to her age.

Joshua's chin dropped, and he focused on the rug at his feet. "He took far too much after my father and grandfather. He loathed my grandmother's paltry—his word, not mine—

existence. As soon as he was old enough, he moved permanently to my father's townhouse and began learning everything he needed to know in order to take over my father's title when the time came."

"Yet, you remained here."

"Until I left for Oxford—at my uncle's insistence—yes." He chuckled. "Despite my brother being the heir apparent, I was the lucky one. My grandmother hired the finest tutors, we visited every museum within a day's carriage ride, and I learned to care for myself. Not every man is given such a gift."

There was much Kate had presumed to know of the solicitor, yet startlingly little of it fit into this new understanding of the man.

He cleared his throat. "My apologies, Miss Kate. I did not intend to burden you with my family situation." His weak smile told her that he had more he wished to share, but thought he'd said enough for the time being.

Kate longed to know more, craved a deeper connection to someone, something to help break away from the solitude she'd shrouded herself in.

"I sent my driver to appraise the damage to your building. The fire was contained on the first floor, the schoolroom for the most part, but was put out rather quickly. The flooring and two walls, as well as the front window and door, will need repairs. The smoke and soot left a mess, but your personal possessions were mostly unharmed."

Only a single night spent in Joshua's house, and Kate had nearly forgotten the travesty awaiting her in Cheapside. "Can we go see the building this morning?"

"Of course."

Her hands trembled, and she set the plate aside before she spilled crumbs all over the expensive blue bedding. "The children...they will be worried."

"Do not fret. I sent word to my assistant, Henry, to speak with each of the children as they arrived to make certain they knew you are well."

He'd thought of everything. "Thank you, my lord."

"Joshua."

"Thank you, *Joshua*." Kate swallowed, heat creeping up her cheeks at the use of his given name despite how often she'd thought of him as simply Joshua, not Mr. Stuart. "You have done too much. I am sorry to have burdened you with all of this. Please, have the physician send his bill to me."

"It is what friends do. And the doctor has been taken care of." He smiled shyly.

Kate had been relegated to a point where she needed another to care for her needs. It was a position she'd promised herself she would never be in. Yet, what other option did she have? She'd never seen a proper physician and had little notion of their fees, but the bill was likely more than what was left of the funds she'd received a few days prior.

"I will return the money as soon as I am able." It was no wonder her father had liked and trusted the solicitor. He'd come to her aid, knowing she had no resources to repay him. And he'd called her friend. "Are we friends?"

Her cheeks flamed hotly at her bold question, while Joshua's eyes widened before his eyelids lowered slightly. "I have always believed so, Miss Kate. Though if you have enough friends and do not wish to add me, I will rescind the offer."

Kate laughed, her chest aching. Friends. Only friends. She'd be a fool to believe that there could be anything more between them. However, counting him as a friend was more than Kate should expect. "One can never have too many friends. Especially ones such as yourself, Joshua."

"As I said last night, I was only in the right place at the right time." He glanced toward the door, his unease apparent. Kate also realized the inappropriate nature of their conversation—especially alone in her bedchambers. Her temporary room in *his* house. "I had my driver collect a fresh gown from your dressing closet. I apologize that I haven't any stowed away here. If you'd like to wash up and dress, I will have my carriage brought round to take us to your schoolroom."

Joshua gave her a curt bow and exited the room, leaving her alone with her chest fluttering.

Could the flutter be a result of the smoke from the fire?

No, it most certainly was not.

She stared at the closed door, a vision of Joshua standing on the landing at her home filling her mind, the man backlit by flames and smoke. Yet, the image couldn't be as it had actually happened. In her daydreams, Mr. Stuart—no, Joshua—was not wearing a shirt, and his intense stare never left her.

Kate shook her head as her father's warning on such wayward thinking filled her with guilt.

Surprisingly, even to Kate, she realized the feeling was in no way accompanied by the remorse that generally followed.

CHAPTER 5

KATE REMOVED HER elbow from the surface of the pristine table linens and folded her arms in her lap, only to bring her hands to rest on the table once more as a door swung open to reveal a procession of three servants. The trio glided through the breakfast room with more poise and grace than Kate had ever managed in her short nineteen years. They held their serving dishes at precisely the same height as their skirts swooshed about their legs. One thing Kate noticed was that their half boots did not make a sound on the gleaming wood floor.

Unlike hers as she'd attempted to slip into the room without drawing Lord Stuart's notice. Her heel still slapped the floor when she walked. Thankfully, most of the walk through his townhouse had been down hallways and stairs lined with plush, vibrant rugs that muffled the sound.

How was it possible that she felt more out of place here in this lovely, airy breakfast room overlooking the townhouse's back gardens than she had when they were alone in her borrowed chambers the night before?

Clasping her hands in her lap once more, Kate leaned back as one of the maids sat a steaming bowl of porridge on the table next to a plate of ham. There was also toast and jam, as well as a pot of tea, and what Kate suspected was cocoa.

At the head of the table, Joshua watched her intently, making Kate all the more nervous.

"Tea, miss?"

Kate jumped in her seat, not realizing a maid stood next to her, her question spoken in a calm, even tone.

"Umm…" She glanced at the table and reached for the finely painted teacup and saucer. As she took hold of it, her fingers shook, causing the cup to clatter against its base. Kate paused, took a shallow breath, and then held it in as she grasped the handle in a firm hold. "Yes, please." She exhaled.

She wasn't used to being served, except for the few times she and her parents had journeyed to the inn down the street from their building. And that had been many years ago when she was still in the schoolroom.

When the maid paused to pour Joshua's cup, he shook his head and dismissed her with a soft smile that Kate had seen him use with her students on many occasions. The other servants trailed after, and they closed the door behind themselves, leaving Kate alone with Joshua once more.

"I hope you slept well." He collected the platter of meats and held it out to her. When she shook her head. he shrugged and started to pile his plate with the delicious-smelling ham. "I can say with almost certainty that the stench of smoke and burnt wood will likely never be removed from my jacket."

Kate was uncertain what the correct response to his declaration was. Should she apologize and offer to replace the garment? Or commiserate with him regarding the likely ruination of her favored nightshift. as well?

Thankfully, he continued before she had time to decide.

"Between you and I." he said. dropping his voice low and glancing around the room as if to verify that they were. indeed. alone. "I despised that coat. The collar was scratchy at my neck. and the sleeves were a half-inch too short. Not to mention the uselessness of the shallow pockets. It is my valet who thought the thing 'the height of fashion.' Mayhap I should have made him wear the dreadful thing for a few hours."

Kate nearly caught herself laughing but held it in, preferring only an amused grin at this jest. The coat had likely cost more than her entire wardrobe. and it was her fault that it had gotten ruined. Besides. if she laughed, it would pain her chest as it had earlier when she coughed. The maid who'd come to tidy her room had assured Kate that she'd overheard the physician say the cough was from the smoke she'd sucked in escaping the fire and it shouldn't persist more than a day or so.

It was exceedingly odd to think that only the previous evening. she'd wandered about her home alone. too conservative to even stoke the fire. And now. just one day later. Kate was here. sitting at a table with proffered tea. cocoa. and farther down the surface, blocked by a centerpiece of soft peach blossoms, a pot of coffee. Kate could smell the earthy, nutty aroma of a blend much akin to that offered by the bookseller in Cheapside.

And she and Joshua were speaking of ruined garments.

This was far removed from her normal morning conversations regarding the children's time spent with family while Kate dwelled on her solitude.

"I have arranged for my carriage to be readied within the hour so we may go directly to Cheapside." Joshua used his utensil to place a perfectly cut piece of ham into his mouth. After chewing for several moments, he swallowed and continued. "I am certain you are anxious to see your building. Quite frankly, I am, too."

"Yes," Kate mumbled. She collected a piece of toast and scooped porridge into her bowl. "I cannot imagine what I will do if everything is lost."

Everything...what little was left from her parents. They'd lived simply, possessing only what they needed and giving the rest away, but there were still things that held great emotional value. Her mother had not gifted her much, but there was a quilt, a beaded bracelet, and a poem she'd scribed for Kate one Christmastide. Losing them in the blaze would wound Kate greatly.

Insignificant items, yet meaningful—if only to her.

"My man says the second floor is easily reachable. We shall be able to search for your possessions as long as we do not linger."

We? Kate kept her eyes focused on her plate, though her thoughts were on Joshua.

No one had ever taken such an interest in her or her schoolroom. Most of her students' parents hadn't so much as even visited their children's classroom.

"We have spent some time together, but I find I know little of you and your family," Joshua mused.

Kate would not share that there were many times *she* felt as if she did not know much of her parents. They'd loved one another and their church, and they'd certainly been devoted to Kate and her well-being. Yet, devotion and love are two very different things in a practical sense.

Love was strong.

Devotion was intense—a responsibility, a duty, a burden.

"I mean to say, when they were with us, I enjoyed chatting with your father regarding many things. In fact,"—Joshua chuckled softly, setting his fork aside—"I believe it was he who insisted the Americans, with their religious ideology, would be the first to throw themselves at our mercy. And…heavens, what would he think of Napoleon being sent to St. Helena?"

Kate's heart ached at the many small things she'd let go about her parents: her father's love of political matters despite his commitment to the church, and her mother's love of pastries, though her father called it gluttonous and sinful when her mother wasn't listening.

"He did relish a rousing political sparring match," Kate said.

"He certainly did. Do you remember the evening I came around and your father insisted I remain until he listed all of Henry VIII's greatest feats?" Joshua poured coffee into his cup and added sugar and a healthy amount of milk to the brew. "I remember feeling envious of you being sent to bed."

"And I'd longed to stay up and take part in

the conversation." Kate admitted.

Joshua's eyes widened. "You know of Henry VIII, too?"

"Heavens, no." Kate said. "I do not much care for the old king; however, I found it rather intriguing when my father grew passionate about a subject."

Kate fell silent. The vicar hadn't been fervent about anything to do with his daughter except insisting a pious, private lifestyle. It was a connection Kate had longed to share with her father, but he'd always kept her just out of reach. And Kate was uncertain why. In her youth, she'd believed it was because she was a mere girl. But as she grew older, she'd come to accept it was more than that, and something that would likely never change.

"Please, forgive me, Kate." Joshua said softly. "I did not mean to cause you unrest."

Kate lifted her gaze to meet his, blinking several times to clear her vision.

"You did not upset me." she confessed. And he hadn't: he'd only stirred feelings within her she'd suppressed for years. Without seeing her parents' stark detachment every day, Kate had been able to dwell on the loving moments, the truly close moments they'd shared as a family. Unfortunately, those times were not nearly as numerous as she'd deceived herself into believing. "It is only that I cannot claim to know my parents any more than you, my lord."

"Why do you say that?" Joshua leaned slightly forward, and a spiced-mint aroma floated toward Kate.

She swallowed, bringing her thoughts back to the conversation—a topic she'd never discussed with anyone. "They were my parents, certainly, but they never spoke to me regarding important matters. Or about themselves. I only knew both sets of grandparents were deceased, and both my mother and father were only children. They wed young, my father being twenty and my mother only sixteen, and they weren't blessed to give their love to a child until later in life."

To distract him from the topic, Kate shrugged and set about spreading jam on her toast.

Joshua must have sensed her unease as he turned his attention once more to his plate.

They ate in companionable silence for a stretch before the quiet in the room became too much for Kate. Her mind ran in circles in times such as these. She thought far too deeply into subjects she did not wish to dwell on, and the energy wasted would all be for naught because she'd still find no answers.

"While my sense of aloneness is greater now."—Kate sighed—"it has always been present. I always noticed that I was different: as did many of the children in my mother's school and in my father's parish."

Her skin tone wasn't that of a normal English girl, her hair did not lay in large, bouncing curls but tight ringlets, and her eyes were not the muddy brown of both her parents. Everyone around them had taken note, especially Kate.

"I think in that regard we are much alike."

Joshua's words surprised her. How could the son of a duke feel alone or different? He'd been raised as part of the peerage, a class above Kate. He could afford things she never could. He was surrounded by servants, Dolly, and the man from his office.

"How can you feel different?"

"My desires for my future contrast greatly with those of my family." He sat back in his chair, his plate empty and his cup drained. "I've set myself apart from them, and that has led to a very lonely existence, especially since my uncle's and grandmother's passing. I do not feel I belong among the *ton,* nor can I truly be a member of Cheapside. It is a position I accept, though."

"My lord." A footman entered the room, stopping to give a quick nod to Kate before addressing Joshua once more. "Your carriage is ready to depart."

"Thank you, Smithe." Joshua pushed back his chair and stood. "Miss Kate, please finish your meal at your leisure. I have a few things to gather in my study before we go. I will meet you in the front hall when you are finished."

With a grin and a bow, Joshua departed the room, following after Smithe.

Kate had had much the same experience as he. She felt as if she didn't belong in the place she'd spent her entire life. Certainly, for different reasons than his, but still, they shared a mutual solitude and a sense of not entirely belonging. Perhaps Joshua *did* understand her situation better than she imagined.

Glancing at her nearly empty plate, Kate knew she shouldn't linger. She needed to see the damage to her building firsthand and decide how to handle it all.

CHAPTER 6

JOSHUA STOOD IN the street outside his office, Kate by his side, as they both stared at her damaged schoolroom. The front window had been shattered in the fire brigade's haste to extinguish the flames. The front door was missing, and Joshua had his driver and stable hand nailing wooden planks to the opening to keep vagrants out. Next, they would cover the large window. Through the gaping hole where the window had been, Joshua took in the burnt desks and ruined books.

The flames, thankfully, hadn't damaged the building beyond repair or traveled much farther than the ground floor. However, Joshua was certain Kate did not possess the funds necessary to fix the building.

"You can stay at my townhouse until the building is safe again," he offered. He turned slightly to find Kate assessing him, her cheeks rosy despite the cool breeze.

When she refocused on the schoolroom, Joshua fought the urge to take her hand and reassure her that all would be well—hopefully, in the not too distant future.

Joshua had no right to promise her anything, but at least in his home she would be safe, cared for, and fed.

Dolly, bless her kind soul, would see to that.

And he wouldn't need to worry incessantly over Cuttlebottom. He'd thought on the matter of the cobbler all night. There was no proof he'd set the blaze, and the simple fact that he'd left his shop and headed down the alley on the far side of the schoolroom would not be enough to urge the authorities to take a closer look at the matter. It was possible the fire had been started by less nefarious means.

The cobbler was an established businessman in Cheapside and had been a close friend of the vicar's, while Kate was a single woman without the benefit of a husband to seek retribution on her behalf. That did not mean Joshua did not plan to see Kate's wrongs made right, and her building whole once more no matter who or what was responsible for setting the blaze.

Kate crossed her arms over her chest. Her demeanor had been the same all morning—confusion mixed with uncertainty. "I cannot ask that of you, my lord. I haven't any notion how long it will take or if I'm capable of repairs at all. Mayhap it would be best to sell what is left of the building to Mr. Cuttlebottom and be done with it all."

Never would Joshua allow the beast to profit from Kate's loss. Though the time was not right to worry her with his suspicions.

"I will assist you with the repairs." Joshua

clasped his hands behind his back as if the task were as simple and easily completed as that. "My stable hand, driver, and I will be at your disposal until the schoolroom is restored. Until that point, you may continue teaching in my building. The back office, while cramped with all the children in attendance, should suit well enough."

"Joshua—ummm—my lord," she said, brushing at her cheek. "I haven't the coin for the repairs. Even with your help, it is a fruitless endeavor. And your office...I cannot repay you for its use."

"Never you mind." He brushed off her concern. "I can work in the front room of the building, and I have some savings—"

"No," she cut off his words. "If I agree to remain at your townhouse and use your office for my schoolroom, I shan't take your money. It is too much. And I do not wish to impose on your kindness."

"Please, allow me to finish." If anyone would understand Joshua's position, it was Kate. "I do not have much saved, certainly not enough for all the repairs needed. However, it will be a start. Mayhap you can contact the individual who sends you money every few months."

Joshua adjusted his cravat, hoping to dispel the awkwardness that had settled between them over his generous offer. They'd never spoken of the parcels he delivered to her. In fact, he'd mistakenly opened one a few years back before realizing it was not addressed to him. That was the only way he knew they contained money.

In the world of the *ton*, it was garish and uncouth to discuss matters such as finances with anyone but your man of business and perhaps your steward. Again, Joshua was reminded of how different his upbringing was compared to his chosen life in Cheapside. Certainly, he could have taken to a life of the *beau monde* and wiled away his allowance and time at the racetrack or White's while spending his evenings in fashionably crowded ballrooms.

"It might be possible for your benefactor to advance you the funds for the repairs," he prodded.

Her lips pursed, and her discomfort visibly grew. "I do not think that is a good idea."

"Why ever not?" he asked. "If you'd like, I can draft the request on your behalf."

She shook her head. "I am unaware who sends the money. We have never met nor communicated in any way except for the envelopes I receive. There is never any correspondence included with the funds."

For not the first time, Joshua was plagued by his own lackadaisical handling of the situation. "You do not know whom the stipends are from?" He'd assumed Kate's mother or father had spoken of the quarterly bequeathals before their deaths.

Keeping her eyes trained on the schoolroom, she said, "The first envelope arrived not long after my father's death. I was so overwhelmed and blessed to have the money, I did not question who'd sent it. I'd even convinced myself for a time that it had come from my father's parishioners or, mayhap, one of my students. I feared if I questioned the origin of the money, it would stop coming. I know it sounds silly—and frankly, feeble-minded on my part— however, I was barely able to keep food in my stomach and was ready to close the school when it arrived. I did my best to make the funds last for as long as possible, but then you delivered another envelope. And another, and another…"

"And, suddenly, it was not so important who your benefactor was." It hadn't mattered overmuch to Joshua either—curiosity aside—when his uncle had charged him with the task of delivering the envelopes. "You are not feeble-minded at all."

She lifted her chin and turned toward him, a spark of defiance in her blue-grey eyes. "It didn't matter as long as I was able to keep my mother's school open, and the children had a safe place to come and learn." She sighed, and Joshua noticed a bit of her fortitude flee. "I know it was wrong to keep accepting the money; however, I justified taking it because I was not benefiting from it—my pupils were. I traded lessons for eggs, milk, and fabric. Some children, born to more blessed families, paid me in coin, which I used for other necessities."

Joshua held her hard stare, making sure she saw understanding in his eyes. "You have done nothing wrong, Kate. The parcels are left at my office, and since your father's death, they have come addressed to you. The money is meant for you. Of that, I have no doubt."

"Who do they come from?" she asked. "And how does this benefactor know my family? Surely, you must know."

"I am uncertain, as well." He regarded the building across the street once more. "I have been delivering them to your family since I finished at Oxford and came to London to work with my uncle. I always assumed you knew who they were from and never wished to pry into such a private matter. My uncle's instructions were to deliver the envelopes and ask no questions. Confidentiality between a solicitor and his client is paramount."

A small girl, dressed in a pink pinafore with

scuffed black half boots and bouncing blond curls skipped down the street. Children came and went from the schoolroom so often that Joshua was not familiar with them all. But when the little girl stopped in front of Kate's building and looked up at the shattered window and the covered doorway, he suspected that she was a pupil of Kate's.

"Lily," Kate called. When the girl turned, Kate waved and looked both ways before crossing the street to greet the child.

She knelt before Lily, embracing the girl before drawing back with a smile. How Kate remained positive with her students despite everything that'd happened was beyond him. Joshua was too far away to hear their conversation, but when Lily's smile turned into a frown, he suspected Kate had told the girl the schoolroom would need repairs before they could begin lessons again.

He hoped that Kate accepted the use of his office to continue with the children.

Kate stood and nodded back in the direction the girl had come skipping from. Lily walked away, likely back home, her shoulders slumped.

Chapman had confided to Joshua that all the children had taken the news of the fire in a similar fashion. Their upset was a clear testament to Kate's skill as a teacher. When Joshua had been young, he'd relished the days his tutors had called off ill or were otherwise indisposed. He'd spent the days lost in far more interesting and exciting things—at least his boyhood self had thought them far more appealing than lessons.

He marveled, not for the first time, how Kate was unlike any other woman in his acquaintance. He had not met a more selfless woman, one who thought of more than their appearance, social status, and what event they'd next attend. What would London be if more of the *ton* worried about others and less about themselves?

Miss Katherina Elliott was not only beautiful on the outside, but she possessed a rare heart of gold. Her curling, ebony hair and striking, almond-shaped, bluish-grey eyes were captivating. And Joshua hadn't been surprised to discover that there was far more to the woman than met the eye.

If his grandmother were alive, Joshua imagined she'd love Kate and admire everything about her as much as Joshua did.

By the time Kate returned to his side, Joshua had decided on a course of action she'd be unable to refuse.

CHAPTER 7

KATE PEERED OUT the window of Joshua's enclosed carriage at a building that made her Cheapside schoolroom appear barely inhabitable—and downright primitive. They'd journeyed from Cheapside to Bond Street and turned onto a well-maintained cobblestone road lined with shops and offices with broad windows, gas lampposts, and door latches of polished silver. She knew they were polished because she'd seen a man in uniform scrubbing at one until it shone. The roadways were not marred by filth or rubbish, and the lords and ladies who walked the street were dressed in gowns fancier than Kate could ever dream of possessing.

She imagined this was what the most proper and wealthy Englishmen and women donned for dazzling balls. But for promenading in the streets? It seemed overdone and senseless, not to mention wasteful and highly unconventional. The grime on the London breeze from the millions of chimneys in town was enough to tarnish any fine silk or satin. When she was younger, her mother had taken in laundry as a way to earn extra coin. Kate had spent many hours scrubbing dresses to remove the soot.

Besides, how did these ladies accomplish anything if they took hours to merely dress and style their hair for the day?

The Stuart driver, Mr. Chapman, climbed down from his perch and pulled open the carriage door with a grand flourish that nearly made Kate giggle.

Attached to the overhang outside the building directly in front of their carriage hung a plaque engraved with the same, *Stuart and Lords, Solicitors*. It was not like the simple shingle that swung on rusted hooks in front of Joshua's Cheapside office.

No, this was the type of building Kate could picture a grand lord doing business in, far removed from the working class who populated her neighborhood.

Through the massive front windows that reached from nearly the ground to the first-floor roofline, Kate watched finely dressed men hurrying to and fro. A servant in a tailored uniform, different from the man polishing the latches, opened the front door, and a couple exited; the man's uneven step supported by a cane with a large, shining emerald jewel mounted to the top. A woman young enough to be his daughter—if not granddaughter—grasped tightly to his arm. However, the way the man held her close to his side and whispered in her ear was not that of a fondness shared between father and daughter.

Joshua stepped from the carriage. The couple issued him a hearty greeting before they continued down the street to their waiting coach, and Joshua turned and held up his gloved hand for her to take.

Her fingers shook as she took in the proffered palm, knowing his hold would be tight and supportive in a way Kate *needed* in that moment. She could depend on Joshua, no matter what came their way. When she stared down into his eyes, she felt a connection that went beyond their friendship. It was something…more.

However, at no time in the last twenty-four hours had Kate felt more out of place than she did in that moment. Not even when she'd awoken in Joshua's fine house, garbed in a nightgown that did not belong to her, and learned he was the son of a duke. Not when he'd offered his assistance to help her repair her home, or when he'd insisted she use his Cheapside office as a makeshift schoolroom until hers was ready. She hadn't even felt peculiar when she learned Joshua had sent his driver and stable hand into her home to collect some of her personal possessions.

Only now, when presented with his outstretched hand as if she were a titled lady, did Kate realize how much Joshua's world, his upbringing and his life, were removed from her own. The differences must be apparent to everyone but Joshua as he smiled up at her.

And Kate did not need to glance down at the sagging heel of her boot to understand the stark reality of their mismatched pairing.

Yet, she'd been unable to fully grasp the lifeline he offered after she'd seen Lily on her way home. Joshua had mused that if his uncle had set up the delivery of her money, it would stand to reason he'd have record of it at his Bond Street office. Which meant, somewhere on the other side of the towering glass façade, Kate could find answers she hadn't realized she longed for.

It had never escaped Kate's notice, or that of those who lived in Cheapside, that she did not resemble either of her parents. Neither the vicar nor his wife had possessed any memorable traits in their appearances. Both had grey hair, brown eyes, and fair, albeit weathered, skin. Neither had been overly tall or remarkably short. In fact, they'd blended in with everyone else in Cheapside. Unlike Kate with her creamy complexion akin to the brown sugar her mother had sprinkled sparingly on her porridge, her long, thick, curly ebony hair, and her almond-shaped eyes. Her father had affectionately dubbed them *enchanting*. When Kate had turned her pleading stare on him, he nearly always gave in to her wishes. Her mother had jokingly called her their *little temptress*, and though the moniker galled her father, she'd noticed that he smirked each time her mother used the affectionate name.

Apart from their unique appearances, one would have to be daft not to notice that her mother had been much too old to have given birth to Kate. Even as a child, she remembered her father's frailty and her mother's wrinkled, sagging skin.

Though it did nothing to deter Kate's utter adoration of the pair.

She'd known from a young age that she was blessed far beyond most in London.

"Miss Kate?" Joshua wiggled his fingers. "Is something amiss?"

She wanted to ask if he had the time for her

to recite her ever-growing list of things that were *seriously* amiss of late; including but not limited to her newfound awareness of him. She'd been in his home, his office, and had met those closest to him. He was no longer the kind solicitor who worked across the street. He was now the man who'd helped her in her darkest hour, saved her from perishing, and gave her hope that life would someday return to normal.

Yet, Kate was acutely aware that nothing would return to their previous normal. The old ways could not exist any longer—at least not for Kate.

She took Joshua's proffered hand, ignoring the heat she felt through their gloves, and stepped from the carriage, satisfied she'd stilled the quiver in her fingers.

When Joshua tucked her hand into the crook of his elbow and pulled her close—not as close or as intimately as the couple who'd greeted him a moment before—Kate was aware how ill-fitting and weathered her gown was with its threadbare elbows and stained, fraying hem. She was satisfied her sagging heel did not slap the ground loudly as she walked, utterly betraying her position on his arm.

To his credit, Joshua did not seem to notice her attire as he nodded to the livery servant as he opened the door, and they entered the building. It was as if they accompanied one another regularly and not only due to the damage of her home. It was a sensation Kate was oddly at ease with, despite her *unease* with her lackluster appearance. Joshua seemed to neither mind nor care—and she appreciated that fact. Their strides mirrored one another's as he set the pace.

Inside, clerks and clients alike halted to greet Joshua and incline their heads to her when introduced—as a client of Stuart and Lords. Again, guilt swamped her at the thought of the expense of such an association with Joshua. The amount would be far more significant than she could ever hope to repay.

They made their way deeper into the building, and Kate leaned close to whisper, "Do all these gentlemen work for you?"

Joshua chuckled, the deep rumbling growing from his chest in the same way her father's laughter had when she surprised him with one of her impetuous questions. She knew it came from his heart. "Some, yes. Others hold similar positions as solicitors, hence the name, Stuart and Lords."

"Oh," she mused, unable to think of a suitable reply that would not betray her bewilderment as they traversed the crowded office.

"After my uncle passed, I brought on many gentlemen similar to myself who studied law and desired the benefit of a steady income and fulfilling work. Now, there are eight solicitors, including myself, and we each own an equal share of Stuart and Lords."

"Which allows you to work from your office in Cheapside?"

"Very good, Miss Kate." He nodded and drew up short before a door at the rear of the large building. "My income from Stuart and Lords enables me to help those with fewer means in Cheapside."

She longed to ask why he would choose to work in Cheapside when he could just as easily help people from this grand office in the safer part of London. If her father had been offered a more prestigious congregation, would he have forsaken his parish in Cheapside? What of her mother? She'd been intelligent enough to seek a position as a proper tutor for an English family; however, she'd remained at her husband's side and taught children who might have otherwise not been afforded an education.

More to the point, what would Kate have chosen if she'd had the means to seek out a better future than her parents had given her?

She'd like to believe she would still be exactly where she was—not in Joshua's upmarket office, but in Cheapside, living and working in the building her mother and father had worked hard to obtain and leave to their only daughter.

"When I began taking on other solicitors, it was necessary for my assistant to consolidate my uncle's records. However, nothing of import was discarded. If a record of your benefactor exists, it will be in here." He pushed open the door, and a clerk followed them into the room, lighting several wall sconces and pulling back the drapes that covered the small window in the back wall. "The files are arranged by year for past clients. And within each year, by name."

"Do you know how long the parcels have been coming?" she asked, taking in the large room with row after row of shelves that reached the ceiling. The room was larger and held more paper than Albert's Bookshop. She'd been visiting the bookseller since she'd learned to read and still had yet to explore every section. A room this size could easily take decades to scour.

When Joshua didn't respond, she glanced up at him as he nodded to the clerk, who departed the room, leaving the door ajar in his wake.

"As long as I can remember," he replied once they were alone. "Four years, at least. Which is when I began working for my uncle."

"I know my parents moved to London shortly after I was born"—she'd nearly said *after I came to live with them,* but that was information she'd only recently been able to speak with Joshua about, and she wasn't certain if she was prepared to speak further on the matter—"and my father took over the vicarage. Originally, I thought the funds came from his congregation."

"That is a good enough place to begin," he mused, rubbing his chin as he scanned the room. "Sometime between five and nineteen years ago. I suppose my idea to arrange the files in such a manner was not my brightest notion."

She laughed, the task ahead of them daunting. "There must be shelf after shelf of files."

"On the contrary." He started through the room, headed toward the shelving unit closest to the back wall and the light streaming in from the window. "During that time, it was only my uncle and his two assistants. Every once in a while, he brought me in to help with menial tasks. Now, if it had been in the past four years, we'd need to enlist the help of every Stuart and Lords clerk."

Joshua began removing boxes from shelves and stacking them on a desk in the corner. It took Kate a few minutes to realize he was pulling all the boxes labeled with an *E*.

For *Elliott*.

The man had taken an insurmountable task—at least, in Kate's opinion—and reduced it to under twenty boxes. He narrowed it down even further when he opened the lids of a few, retrieved a folder to review, then shook his head and slid the boxes back on the shelf. She could not take her eyes off him as he moved swiftly through the room, the muscles under his coat and along his back straining as he worked. His movements required more strength and agility than she suspected your average solicitor possessed. The shelves were stacked to the ceiling, and he often needed to climb onto the wooden racks to retrieve a box. And all of it was accomplished without breaking a sweat nor removing his jacket. She could certainly see why he'd felt qualified to offer his assistance with the schoolroom.

"You are very accomplished with the way the files are stored." It was as close to a compliment as she could come without mentioning the *accomplished* way he pulled himself up onto the shelves and then jumped down, all without spilling the contents of a single box or wrinkling the fabric of his shirt and jacket where it pulled tightly across his shoulders. And she would not dare allow herself to ponder the fit of his trousers that were at eye level during his many climbs. They were at his office to discover the secrets of her past, yet Kate found it rather difficult to suppress her need to explore Joshua's secrets.

His brow rose as if he'd read her musings. "You cannot think my uncle made it so easy for me to earn my place in his office, Miss Kate."

She very nearly sighed with relief. They'd been speaking of his uncle.

She gave him an overzealous smile, thinking back to what she knew of Michael Stuart. He'd been friendly, jovial, and had arrived at the parish or the schoolroom regularly as if he offered her father friendship, as well as serving in a more official capacity. To Kate, he had only been known as her father's friend, Michael, not as a solicitor, and certainly not as *my lord*.

"When I was seven, I was charged with sweeping the office. By twelve, I'd gained enough knowledge from my uncle that he allowed me to transport missives and documents to and from the courts. Before I departed for Oxford to obtain my proper law education, he gave me the task of researching different laws for him." Joshua pulled out the desk chair and gestured for her to sit. "There is no task at Stuart and Lords I have not been assigned to at some point in time. Finding my way around a storage room is one of my best skills."

Kate wanted to share how similar she and Joshua were. They'd both worked tirelessly and gained the skills needed for their chosen professions.

There were still many boxes to search with no guarantee they'd find any useful information that would help them. "Do you truly believe we will find anything?"

"Do not be so glum," he chided with a smile. "If there is a record, with any luck, it will be in one of these boxes."

"Luck," she scoffed, sitting in the chair. "I haven't had much of that of late."

"True," he mused, removing the lids from two boxes. "Then let us put our trust in fate. What fortune does fate gain by allowing a fire to ravish your schoolroom and leave you homeless?"

Kate laughed if only to suppress the sorrow that coursed through her. Since awakening at Joshua's townhouse, she hadn't allowed herself to wallow in self-pity or dwell on everything she'd lost in the fire. "You forgot, penniless."

"If we find what we are looking for, my hope is that you won't be penniless for long."

"You have more optimism than I can muster, at least in my situation." She focused on the files he'd stacked in front of her, thumbing through the folders. Easton. Edgewood. Edmonds. Elmer. Eskins. Ewing.

No Elliott.

She set the files aside and removed the lid from the next box.

"If you keep the faith, fortune always follows." He returned another box to its place on the shelf.

The son of a duke was far more likely to find fortune than a woman born in Cheapside. Fortune was practically bred into men of the upper class. Joshua's idea of faith and Kate's view on it were very different. Faith was something that allowed her people to make it through long, stormy nights with no heat and little to eat, knowing that tomorrow would bring nothing different than the day before. Still, those of the working class raised themselves from their flea-ridden beds, dressed in their worn clothes, and trudged through their day, only to return to their beds hungry and cold once more the next night.

She shook her head to clear her maudlin, dour thoughts.

What would her father say if he were alive to witness her *faithless* musings?

Besides, Joshua could no more be held accountable for the circumstances surrounding his birth than she was.

They were both fortunate in their own ways.

"Ah-ha!" Joshua held a folder above his head. "Here it is. And in record time."

He placed the file on the table in front of her and retreated.

"Go ahead, look at it," he prodded.

Kate glanced over his shoulder, wishing she felt even a small measure of the excitement clearly shining in his expression. She was uncertain what was worse: not finding the file they sought, or discovering it didn't hold the answers she longed for.

She ran her fingers along the edge of the file and over the word: *Elliott/De Vere – Via Mr. Caleb Abelston, Solicitor (The Duke and Duchess of Shrewbury)*.

Except for her own surname, she recognized none of the others.

She reread the label, praying something would spark her memory, but…nothing.

She'd never heard the name De Vere, nor was she acquainted with a Mr. Caleb Abelston. And the closest she'd come to meeting a true duke was Joshua, and he was only the second son of a duke.

"I do not know any of these people," she confessed. "What of you?"

"Abelston was my uncle's friend. He passed away not long after I left for Oxford." He stepped forward and reached over her shoulder to flip the file open. His fingers grazed her cheek as he pulled back. "Mayhap there is more information inside."

She swallowed at the same time a shiver ran down her spine. She attempted to forget how close Joshua stood. If she reclined even an inch, her shoulders would touch him. She'd never longed for such an intimate touch with a man before, but in that moment, Kate wanted more, so much more than the mere accidental graze of Joshua's hand.

She wanted the touch to be purposeful and unending, not momentary and unplanned.

Instead of giving in to the urge to think and do something that had nothing to do with her precarious situation, Kate began to read the top page in her parents' file. It held little more than the location of her father's vicarage and their residence above the schoolroom. The next page detailed a schedule of payments made, beginning in April 1803, and continuing quarterly until about a few years ago.

"I was born in December 1802."

"The last scheduled payment recorded was the month before my uncle's passing."

"We were correct in our assumptions," she said, pointing at the date at the top of the page. "My parents said they moved to Cheapside from the countryside a couple of months after I was born. This is dated February 1803."

"Mayhap it is linked to your father's vicarage?"

"I do not think so," Kate replied, flipping to the next page. "What would a duke have to do with an impoverished vicarage in Cheapside?"

"Not his Cheapside appointment, but his past one…in the country. Did he ever speak of where it was or what shire they moved from?"

She shook her head. "My parents preferred not to speak of the past."

She had believed that her parents had suffered through a miscarriage, and that was why they doted on her and were overly concerned with her safety. They'd treated her as if she were as fragile as a perfectly sculpted statue. And as valuable, as well.

The next page listed several names and a direction:

The Duke and Duchess of Shrewbury
Pierce De Vere, Earl of Holderness
Shrewbury Gardens
Oxfordshire, England

As she set the paper aside, a smaller slip of

parchment fell from the file. Across the top was written *Bank of England* with a date listed as February 1803. It was a recorded deposit for forty-two thousand pounds in a trust account for Vicar Ralph Elliott and his wife Mrs. Mercy Elliott. The funds were to be given out quarterly for a twenty-one-year period, with an initial withdrawal of ten thousand pounds. Kate's hand trembled. She received four hundred pounds every three months.

Twenty-one years from February 1803 would be February 1824—two years away. Part of her was relieved to know how long she had to keep receiving the funds, while the rest of her wished to return to the time when she gladly accepted the envelope and never dreamt of the day they would stop coming.

"What does the final paper say?" Joshua's warm breath caressed the nape of her neck and, for a brief moment, Kate focused on his closeness.

Setting the deposit record aside, she looked at the final paper. It was more of a document.

"It is a deed. To a property."

There was no need to find the property location on the document. The deed was dated March 1803, and the sale price was ten thousand pounds.

It was for the schoolroom and her residence above...the only home Kate had ever known.

"It appears we have little option but to seek out the Duke and Duchess of Shrewbury in Oxfordshire." Joshua's matter-of-fact declaration was not in line with Kate's thinking in the slightest. "You and I must remain in London to begin the work on your building. I can send Henry, my assistant, to Oxfordshire with your request."

"Do you not wonder why the duke and duchess would bequeath such a generous amount to my parents?" she stuttered, gathering all the papers. "It is a lot of money, my lord."

"Joshua," he corrected. "And all the paperwork seems to be in order. Does it matter what the money is for?"

"It is more than mere money. It is a *fortune*, Joshua." And it would run out shortly after her twenty-first birthday. She couldn't shake the suspect timing of it all. She had been born, her parents had moved to London, purchased an entire building, and her father worked nearby. She'd always believed that her father's meager salary from the vicarage provided enough for their living expenses. One thing she refused to believe—or spend one more moment pondering—was the notion that her parents were involved with something outside the law and that's where the money had come from. Her father had preached numerous times about the evils of ill-gotten goods. Never would he have accepted payment in reparation for an illicit deed. Would he?

As she shoved everything back into the folder, the backside of one of the pages caught her notice. There was a design scrawled in black ink on the half sheet. It wasn't drawn haphazardly but with care and precision. Something within Kate warmed as she traced the pattern—she'd never seen it before, but she felt it meant something.

The bottom of the page was missing, torn away, leaving the paper half the size of the rest.

She finally turned the document over and set it back in the file and closed the folder.

"I'm sorry, Kate." Joshua settled his hand on her shoulder, and the intimate connection from earlier returned. He hadn't only set about to help her, he was also a part of it all. The defeat in his tone spoke to the fact. "At least we can proceed with contacting the duke. And the deed proves the building belongs to you and no one else."

What had she hoped to find? The money had been arriving for so many years already, it was careless to believe the answers were so readily available to her and Joshua. Kate rested a hand flat on the table atop the file and closed her eyes. Why did it seem that every time she gained some spark of hope it was stripped from her?

"Mayhap I am not meant to discover anything of my past."

Joshua's hand moved down her arm until his hand rested on hers, covering the file even more. "We shall not allow a small setback to dissuade our quest, shall we?"

She turned slightly and glanced up to where he stood behind her. He grinned, and she noted a twinkle in his eyes. The situation was serious and could have dire consequences for Kate, but she nor Joshua was prepared to walk away from it.

Joshua stepped back as she stood and turned to fully face him, the shelves of file boxes at his back. She wanted the truth, yet she also knew that she didn't want to disappoint Joshua if she gave up or if correspondence with the duke proved fruitless.

"Kate." Her name was little more than a sigh escaping his lips as he gazed down at her. "I know it does not seem like much information, but we now know several names and places to continue our search. What more have we to do until your building is repaired?"

She could list a dozen responsibilities between them, the children and his clients at the top of the list.

"It cannot hurt to send Henry with my request," she acquiesced.

He took her gloved hand and squeezed it reassuringly. "I will draft a letter with all due haste and have Henry on his way presently."

Kate stood in stunned silence as Joshua raised her hand and placed a kiss on her wrist, a mere inch above her glove. The heated press of his lips to her bare flesh had her stomach fluttering and her breathing quickening. The gesture was so unexpected a squeak escaped her throat, and she nearly pulled her hand from his hold. But, at the same time, her heart wanted to beg for more.

"Joshua?" She didn't step away as he pulled back and dropped their hands, keeping a hold of her finger. His gaze never left hers. What struck her the most was the way the golden flecks sparkled in his eyes. "I—I—I—"

What she wouldn't give to be fortunate enough to stare into his eyes forevermore.

"My lord?" The door pushed open, flooding the interior of the records room with the light and noise from the outer offices.

She wasn't sure who moved first, but they broke apart as if they'd been caught in a most compromising and scandalous position. His hand released hers, and Kate's chest tightened as the loss of the contact overtook her. But Joshua was not hers, he would never be hers. And as such, he was not hers to lose.

"Good day, Mr. Barber," Joshua greeted the clerk as he stepped into the room.

"I was sent to see if you were in need of assistance." The man stared only at Joshua, and Kate dropped her gaze to her feet.

"We were just finishing up but thank you." Joshua collected the file from the table and held out his arm to Kate. "Are you prepared to depart?"

Every instinct within her screamed that she was not ready to depart, that she needed a few more minutes alone with Joshua...to discover what had transpired between them and intuit what was to come.

However, when Mr. Barber strode into the room and began returning boxes to the shelves and tidying the mess they'd made, Kate knew her moment with Joshua had passed.

With a smile, she took Joshua's arm, and they started for the door.

Kate had been right. The file had only brought about more questions and gave her few—if any—answers. Perhaps it would be the same with her connection to Joshua.

Though she was resigned that if their search proved fruitless, she'd set aside finding out about her past. Kate was not positive that she could do the same where Lord Joshua Stuart was concerned.

CHAPTER 8

JOSHUA CAST A smile to his left and nodded as his footman delivered their final course, dessert. He reached forward and served Miss Kate and then himself. Raspberry tart with a flaky, buttery crust, exactly as his grandmother had perfected decades ago with the help of her own mother. As she grew older and no longer pursued a pastime many called unsuitable for a duchess of her station, his grandmother had taught a few trusted servants to prepare the dessert.

Kate sat rigid in her chair, though her gaze devoured the sweet treat.

"It is as scrumptious as it appears, I assure you," he volunteered in an attempt to break the silence that'd overtaken the room since she'd joined him for last meal. They hadn't had much time following his impromptu kiss of her wrist to speak openly without a servant near. Even Dolly had taken to being close at hand when Joshua and Kate were in residence at his townhouse. "The crust is made with churned butter from the barn out back."

When she did not acknowledge his words, he thought about offering that the raspberries were from his family's country estate, picked from bushes allowed to grow with wild abandon since long before Joshua was born.

It would be for naught, he was afraid.

Kate had been quiet and withdrawn since they returned from his office on Bond Street, and Joshua had summoned Henry to leave for Oxfordshire immediately with the missive he'd drafted for the Duke of Shrewbury. Kate needed funds to complete the repairs. With the vast amount already given to her family, Joshua hadn't thought anything of his request for an additional payment of two thousand pounds to be issued with all due haste.

It would be enough to see the building back to good standing, with enough left to repurchase all the books that had been destroyed and perhaps some supplies to fill Kate's pantry.

She'd thought the amount requested excessive. Yet, he'd explained it was only a starting point.

The art of negotiation was something Joshua knew much about.

He asked for two thousand pounds, and the duke would likely agree to fifteen hundred pounds.

Not as much as they'd asked for, but plenty to see the schoolroom mended so lessons could begin anew.

Joshua knew his father—or his brother— would not so much as sniff at two thousand pounds. It was a paltry sum for most wealthy lords.

And then, perhaps when the matter of finances and repairs were duly in hand, they would have ample time to speak on the subject of what had transpired between them. If Kate wanted to discuss it. Of late, Joshua could not help but wonder if he'd made a grave mistake and manufactured an attraction and bond that did not exist on Kate's part. But he couldn't worry about that right now.

"With luck, Henry will return by tomorrow evening with a note for the funds." Joshua took a bite of his tart and waited for Kate to look up at him. "I will arrange for workers to begin repairs within a fortnight, two at the very most."

"What if the duke refuses your request?" she whispered.

"Then we will manage until your next envelope arrives," he said around another bite of tart. It did not escape his notice that she'd yet to even so much as try the dessert. "You can teach lessons in my office for as long as necessary."

Kate's body tensed further in her chair, and much like their moment in the file room, Joshua wondered if he'd misspoke or misjudged the situation. He could not imagine the pressure and uncertainty that weighed on her, and he only wanted to assist her. In any way he could.

"You have already done too much." Her defeated stare met his. "This is all too much to expect from you. From anyone. If the duke denies my request, I will find the means to complete the repairs."

"I want to help." Unsurprisingly, he meant every word. At some point, he'd begun to think of himself and Kate as a *we,* and the damage to her schoolroom *their* situation—together, not Kate's alone. It had been many years since he'd truly felt in league with another. A true partner.

"We will make the best of the situation. Before we know it, your home will be fixed."

Joshua had other means if the Duke of Shrewbury denied them. He could seek out his father for the funds. He'd asked for nothing from his father or the estate since he turned eighteen and attended Oxford with the assistance of his grandmother. The old man, as disagreeable as he was, could not turn his nose up at such a simple request. It was a paltry amount. Certainly, his father would relish the moment when his independent second son came begging for funds.

"Come now, Kate, you must eat." Joshua scooped another portion of dessert onto his plate, determined not to allow the prospect of possibly seeing his father dim the enjoyment of his meal with Kate. There was no guarantee how long he'd have her in his home, and Joshua planned to make the most of it. "We cannot have Dolly thinking we did not find utter delight in her raspberry tart. She will mourn for days on end."

"My apologies." Her eyes focused on her plate as she took a bite of the tart. "I think I am simply exhausted from it all."

Being left without a home and few possessions was a fate Joshua would never wish on his worst enemy. He'd been grateful to inherit his grandmother's townhouse. What would he have done had he finished school and been made to throw himself on his father's mercy until he established enough coin to find his own lodging? With or without her schoolroom, Kate had nearly no income outside of the small quarterly stipend.

Try as Joshua might, he was never able to be entirely rid of what came with being the son of a duke. He'd never be cast out onto the streets. He'd never need worry about where his next meal would be found. And he'd never be in a position where he was incapable of earning a living.

Title. Wealth. Inheritance. Privilege.

Everything he despised about the aristocracy, yet things he could not cut ties with no matter how much distance he attempted to put between himself and his upbringing.

The trappings of noble birth were much akin to a noose around his neck.

People such as Kate deserved such a life yet were excluded due to their social standing. It was unjust. Those born to wealthy, titled parents had the means to make their way in life, while those who weren't had to fight for necessities like housing, food, and education.

He wanted Kate to feel welcome and safe in his home; however, as their day progressed, especially after finding his uncle's file, she'd only withdrawn more into her shell. He'd thought maybe she worried over residing in his home and had instructed Dolly to act as a chaperone. It had done nothing in the way of putting Kate at ease.

It was as if she'd found something that scared her in those pages, and he'd been too dull to notice.

"It is reassuring to know we hold the property deed to your building." Joshua pushed his plate away, and a footman hurried forward to remove it. Hopefully, a change in topic would pull Kate out of her silence. "I'd meant to ask after it a few days ago, but it slipped my mind."

That was true enough. After he'd gone to see Cuttlebottom and demanded he leave Kate be and stop his quest, he'd all but forgotten about the paper. In truth, Joshua had been doing everything in his power to assist Kate, not only because she was a friend, but also for the fact that he worried the fire was a direct result of his embroiling himself in the situation between the neighbors. If he hadn't gone to the shoemaker, especially after Kate had asked him to leave the situation alone, perhaps Cuttlebottom wouldn't have been sparked into retaliation. If, indeed, the cobbler had anything to do with the blaze.

Joshua should have confessed his possible hand in the fire from the beginning, even knowing very well it could push her away.

No. Once her building was repaired and she had a place to go, he would tell her.

Joshua had made a mess of everything.

"I was worried that my father had made an agreement with Mr. Cuttlebottom, and he possessed the deed."

"Why didn't you tell me?" Joshua asked. "I would have helped you search for it—"

"Where?" she questioned, leaning back in her chair. "Until today, we didn't know a file for my parents existed, nor who was financing my mother's schoolroom. They kept much from me. Why should it surprise me that my father might have given my home away?"

Joshua was struck by her question simply because it was something his father would have done to him if he'd had the upper hand. "You cannot think that way."

"I most certainly can—and do." A new tension brought her upright in her seat, and Joshua noted her anger. "They never thought to speak to me of the money. They never valued me enough to tell me who the mysterious Duke and Duchess of Shrewbury are, or why they decided to move to Cheapside after I was born."

Joshua remained quiet. Sometimes, it was necessary for people to talk, to say all they'd been keeping bottled up inside, and when it was all out, a new peace and rationale would come. He'd spent many years angry at his father, desperate for a meaningful relationship with the man, only to discover time and again that it would never be possible for them.

"Joshua, they left me. Both of them left me to fend for myself, but they did not give me the information I needed to do that. The funds in the account will be depleted soon, and then what shall I do? What if the duke doesn't send what we need? I am without a room to teach the children. Where will they go? Their parents cannot afford proper tutors or a fancy London school." She took in a deep breath before continuing. "What will happen to Sally Ann and the others? I can only pray that their parents see to their future, but what if they do not? What if one of my students is left like me, without the benefit of a home to call their own? Will the girls be forced to wed or sent to a workhouse? The boys…will they turn to pickpocketing and beggary to make their way in the world? If I cannot repair the building, their options will decrease even further. I cannot live with that."

Finally, she slumped back, the intensity and fire leaving her eyes.

Joshua wanted to tell her that everything would work out—he would make sure of it, no matter what he needed to do to accomplish it. It wasn't what Kate needed to hear in that moment. Neither was it something she would accept.

He also suspected that she didn't need someone to *fix* everything for her, though she hadn't told him what she sought from him. Things had shifted after she read the file. No longer was it all about gaining the funds from the duke. It was something more. Joshua didn't understand it, and perhaps he never would. If

Kate were anything like her father, she'd want to forge ahead on her own, see the work completed to her specifications, and not accept his help.

One thing was very clear: Joshua would not stop until everything was set to rights for Kate. Whether that included simply repairing her building and making sure the children resumed their education, or discovering everything that was behind her parents' connection to Shrewbury, Joshua would see it to the end.

If Kate allowed him to be part of it.

They only need wait until Henry returned from Oxfordshire.

After that, they would either have the funds or…

"I think I shall retire." Kate made to stand, and his footman stepped forward to pull her chair back. Every inch of her seemed weighed down by some unseen force, and Joshua desperately wanted to relieve the pressure. Yet, he was bound by what Kate would allow. "Thank you for the meal, and please give Dolly my appreciation for her lovely tart."

She dipped her head, refusing to meet his stare.

"Sleep well," Joshua said, standing. To himself, he wished her a peaceful slumber and a few hours reprieve from everything that weighed on her.

Kate nodded and hurried from the dining hall, her footsteps sounding in the corridor as she fled.

Tomorrow…tomorrow Henry would return to London.

From there, it would be clear how Joshua would need to proceed. They would have money from the duke, or Joshua would set out for his father's townhouse for the first time since he departed for Oxford. A part of Joshua suspected meeting with his father would likely be easier than convincing Kate to accept the money.

Joshua rubbed at his temples as his head started to ache.

Perhaps he needed rest as much as she.

CHAPTER 9

KATE ENTERED HER bedchamber, closing the door in her wake and removing her cloak. Tossing the garment on the bed, she took off her gloves, noting the ash that marred the material before setting them atop her overgarment. The room, with its muted blue hues, dark furniture, and bay windows was meant to be calming and inviting. The issue Kate had found with the space was that it was precisely that…peaceful to the point where she found herself forgetting who she truly was and where she belonged. It had progressed so far and fast that Kate had begun to truly see the room as hers—the gowns in the wardrobe, the clean linens, and the tiny, feminine writing desk…all hers.

This reprieve in Cavendish Square with Joshua was only temporary.

She allowed her bare fingers to trail down the fine fabric of the bedding on the mattress, the material soft to her touch.

She belonged in Cheapside with her pupils, and Joshua belonged in a place like his Bond Street office—or in his fancy townhouse.

Yet, each time she discovered something new of the man, she found herself drawn to him even more. Before it had been something Kate was able to push to the back of her mind, but living and working in such close proximity made that impossible—even more difficult than it had been when she'd had her own residence to reside in. She hadn't been able to truly trust another without reservations since her parents' passing. In her heart, Kate knew Joshua would never betray the trust she'd placed in him. His optimism was unparalleled, and she often wondered where a man gained such confidence that things would work out as dictated.

She slowly spun in a circle. She was faced by a small table holding a pearl-handled brush and comb, a deep wardrobe closet with only her meager belongings inside, and a long, low bookshelf filled with stories Kate had never read. She removed each of the volumes carefully and perused their titles before replacing them on the shelf, making a mental note on a few to see if Albert's Bookshop carried them. She would not fall into the trap of reading any of the books here because there was no way of knowing if she'd be in the room long enough to finish one.

Her living quarters above the schoolroom were nothing compared to Joshua's home. And he moved about the house as if he belonged, while Kate feared tracking soot onto the newly polished floors or spilling her tea on a priceless rug. The thing she'd noted both in her home and his was that they possessed warmth. No matter the size, these walls had seen much love, kinship, and laughter, just as hers had. That feeling only deepened Kate's sense of peace while in Joshua's townhouse.

Their time alone had only further pushed her thoughts and emotions to a place Kate wasn't prepared to explore. She'd barely been able to meet Joshua's stare after he kissed her—even though it had only been her wrist. Her heart had fluttered, and her nights had been filled with images she longed to experience while awake. It made their morning drives to Cheapside all the more uncomfortable for Kate. Could Joshua sense her wanton thoughts? Did he know her pulse raced every time she even so much as thought about his palm caressing her arm to take her hand?

When she wasn't allowing her daydreams to overtake her every thought, Kate was worried about what she'd learned regarding her mysterious benefactor. Or, more appropriately, what she *hadn't* learned from the file.

The Duke and Duchess of Shrewbury.

Pierce De Vere, the Earl of Holderness.

Who were these strangers, and what did they have to do with her past, her family? And, more daunting, how would they impact her future?

It was something she'd wanted to speak to Joshua about, but she was at a loss for how to bring up the matter.

There was no way he could understand how she'd felt all her life, the sense that she hadn't truly belonged. As a part of her family but also an outsider. Not because they treated her as such—or at least Kate hadn't felt such a way until quite recently. It hadn't helped when she discovered that her father might have struck an agreement with Mr. Cuttlebottom to sell her home. That uneasiness and uncertainty had grown and been made worse when she read Joshua's file on her parents. These strangers in Oxfordshire… Her parents hadn't thought her worthy enough to discuss them with her. Had they thought to live long enough the mysterious funds would run out and they'd never have to tell her? Did they think to marry her off to some blacksmith or merchant in Cheapside and the money would no longer be a necessity for her?

Her parents had sheltered her to the point of Kate thinking herself truly breakable. She'd been schooled by her mother alongside the other children in the neighborhood. She'd never been allowed to walk to the bookshop or her father's vicarage without her mother or father at her side. She'd never traveled outside of Cheapside until Joshua had brought her to his townhouse.

The worst part was that she'd accepted it all without question.

She'd trusted and valued her parents enough to never say nay to their decisions and always abide by their rules. It had been so all-encompassing Kate hadn't seen them as rules at all but rather her parents' loving way of guiding her.

In truth, they'd lied to her all these years.

A lie of omission was still very much a lie.

And to make everything worse, the only people who could give her any answers were dead, and there would be no additional money sent.

As long as her mother smiled upon her, and her father held out his hand to her when they walked to his parish, Kate had been happy and content to believe every word they said. Had they spoken of her gullibility while she was fast asleep in the next room? Had they conspired to keep the truth of their and her past from her? Had they thought she'd continue to live in ignorance all her life?

A bit of the adoration she'd carried in her heart all these years slipped away.

To make everything even more confusing, and with her destitute future looming, Henry had brought word that the previous Duke and Duchess of Shrewbury had both passed away— long before Kate's parents. Their heir was not thought to be in England for contact, and for reasons unknown to the servants at Shrewbury Gardens, he hadn't returned to his family home in nearly twenty years. Joshua's assistant had returned from Oxfordshire emptyhanded.

A part of her wondered if she'd been stripped of her ability to find closure at all.

There were answers to be found, somewhere, and Kate was certain it had to do with far more than simply the reasoning behind the mysterious bank deposit and stipend. Had her mother and father resided at Shrewbury before coming to London with her as an infant?

The amount was an exorbitant price to pay a mere vicar and his wife, even if they'd been a part of Shrewbury's staff for generations.

It was more than many in Cheapside earned in their entire life.

And why had her parents come to Cheapside when they could have spent the money on a small cottage in the country and escaped the harsh conditions of the city?

Kate halted, not realizing she'd begun to pace in the room that had quickly begun to feel like her very own after only several days, from the wall of windows to the hearth and then back toward the door. Despite everything that weighed on her, she'd slept soundly each night and had awoken the next morning ready to teach again and assist with her building's renovations.

But this was, by far, her largest problem.

She knew living with Joshua, traveling to Cheapside with him, and teaching in his office were not long-term solutions. Their brief, intimate moment in the file room aside, he was likely being kind to her because he'd known her parents. He was being generous in helping her repair the schoolroom because he was not so crass as to throw a woman onto the streets or deny students an education. He'd rescued her, brought her to his home, and he was without recourse to make her leave.

There was no other explanation for his continued kindness.

Even as the thoughts flooded her with doubt, Kate suspected Joshua's attention and help were not only from kindness. Their connection, while still a new thing Kate was only beginning to comprehend, was undeniable. Sometimes, at their meals, she caught him staring at her when he thought she didn't notice. There were times Kate felt more herself, more *whole* because Joshua was by her side. She hadn't realized something was missing from her life. But now, after her time with Joshua, she knew she would lose a piece of herself if he were gone. Everything about him brought the security Kate had been lacking.

A light knock sounded at the door.

Kate pressed her palms to her heated cheeks, hoping they were not as red as she feared. She sent a small prayer heavenward that she hadn't been reduced to tears.

The knock sounded once more, this time with a bit more urgency.

It was likely Dolly come to collect what

needed to be laundered. It still made Kate uncomfortable to send her garments to a laundress when she was perfectly capable of washing and hanging them to dry herself. Even during the particularly short period when they had extra coin to hire a woman to cook for them, Kate had always washed her own gowns and underpinnings in boiling water with hard-packed soap that her mother had bartered for, and then hung them outside her parents' window that faced the back alley. Depending on the weather, it could take days for a gown to properly dry, but Joshua's servants took her worn gowns, stockings, and gloves and returned them by the next morning. The notion that a servant was made to work while Kate slept increased her sense of guilt over the situation. Having another see to her needs was a concept Kate had yet to accept. It had always been Kate helping others.

And now to have Joshua and his servants currying to her needs? It was difficult, if not impossible for Kate to accept.

"Enter." Kate collected her stained gloves and took in the hem of her gown. The sturdy cotton had collected some filth from her afternoon in the schoolroom but would suffice for another wearing before it needed cleaning. Besides, she only planned to work again tomorrow. "Good evening, Dolly." She kept her back to the door, not yet at ease with the elderly woman's gentleness in both tone and manner. "I think I shall forgo any washing this evening."

Kate hurriedly tucked her gloves into the pockets of her dark cloak to hide the soot-marred fabric.

A deep chuckle rumbled from the doorway.

She pivoted, her cheeks growing ever

warmer when she saw Joshua standing outside her open door. Yet, hadn't she dreamt of just such an occurrence on more than one occasion?

"My lord," Kate exclaimed. "My apologies. I thought it was—"

"Dolly, mayhap?" His smirk made him appear years younger than he actually was, but also belied the awkwardness of his presence in her personal space. "And if you insist on turning away Dolly's treasured duties, it would be best to accept my offer to purchase you a few gowns. I've seen how tirelessly you've been working, and the destruction it is wreaking havoc on your attire. I mean—" He cleared his throat, the humor leaving his tone. "If you would be willing to agree to my offer."

Kate's chin dipped to hide her unexpected smile, it being one of the first times he'd shown any signs of unease, as if he would be devastated if she turned down his offer. Yet, that was precisely what she needed to do. His generosity had swiftly turned Kate's feelings from indebtedness to something more akin to flattery. "I cannot accept any more from you, Joshua. You have already given me too much."

He waved his hand at the room. "A place to sleep, a few meals, and a carriage ride across town? It is hardly anything. And to be honest, I am happy for the company."

The flutter in her stomach returned. She longed to make their living situation permanent, though she had no right to the desire.

He'd done way more for her than he was willing to admit. Earlier that day, a pair of men had arrived to help her clear the debris from the schoolroom in preparation for the repairs. They'd worked alongside her for hours, lifting the heavier desks and shelving until Joshua joined them after completing his work for the day.

Joshua had labored alongside her, and Kate hadn't been shocked at the team they made, working together until they were both exhausted and filthy. The work had been hard; however, the company had been splendid.

"What of Dolly?" Kate asked, banishing the images of Joshua with his shirtsleeves rolled up as they worked. "I am certain she cherishes her time with you."

The older woman acted more akin to a doting mother than Joshua's grandmother's companion. Several times since Kate had been in residence, she'd noted Dolly watching Joshua, keeping an interested eye on the man.

"Dolly tired of me before I reached the age of ten. She would rather retire to her sitting room with a novel or work in the kitchens with Cook than listen to me bore her with tales of paperwork, agreements, settlements, and the like." Joshua stepped into the room, and Kate nodded toward the sitting area close to the hearth. "Thank you. I hope you do not mind if I join you for a bit. I have news."

Kate had grown accustomed to Joshua throughout their arrangement. Even now, she knew once he took his seat, he'd run his hand through his hair, straighten his cravat, and clear his throat before speaking again.

And she was correct. Perhaps at another time, she would have smiled to herself at the accuracy of her guess.

But Kate was uncertain she wanted to hear what he had to tell her.

Conversing in her bedchamber was little different than sharing an enclosed coach on their drive to Cheapside. With anyone else, especially a man, Kate would feel hesitant to be alone. But not Joshua. Her father had trusted him, a rarity for the man, and her mother had never turned the solicitor away when he came to call, even when the vicar was not at home. Both her parents would be eternally grateful for his kindness to Kate, and they'd be disappointed in their daughter if she repaid said kindness by insulting Joshua.

Besides, he was helping her, not seducing her.

The thought sent fresh ideas whirling through her mind: the feel of his lips against her skin, the scent of him freshly washed and shaven for the day, the way his eyes lingered encouragingly on her when she wanted to say something but couldn't find the proper words.

Joshua was helping her, indeed, but a part of her hoped for…

He cleared his throat once more and ran his hands down the front of his trousers where he sat in the large armchair facing the hearth.

Kate perched on the edge of the chaise lounge, afraid to soil the light blue brocade with her dusty skirts as she attempted to rein in her wanton thoughts.

Her head swam as he took her in, his stare moving swiftly down her seated form before settling on her face once more. Could he be entertaining similar notions of attraction? Certainly, he would not have taken her hand and kissed her wrist if he hadn't.

"I have asked around about Pierce De Vere, the current Duke of Shrewbury, previously the Earl of Holderness. But as the servants informed my man, he has not been seen or heard from in many years." He stretched out his legs, crossing them at the ankles before continuing, "I have made inquiries of several solicitor associates to ascertain what they know about the elusive lord and his sire, but all I've heard is that the couple was a bit reclusive in the country, and their son enjoyed the...err, *attention* of many ladies about town."

Kate begged the tension to leave her. It had to be caused by his confession and not the way his gaze on her person made her stomach flip. "Is that so different from other lords of his station?"

Joshua chuckled. "Very wise observation. Are you certain you have not spent more time among the arrogant, pompous men of the *ton*?"

"You are the first and only lord I am acquainted with." Would he care if she had moved among others of his status?

Startlingly, it mattered greatly to Kate if it was important to him.

"I do hope you have garnered your opinion of the upper class based on my example."

"Of course," she stuttered, though he was obviously jesting with her.

They hadn't had a private moment to discuss the news Henry had returned with from Oxfordshire—or, more aptly, Kate had shied away from speaking of it. She suspected Joshua would only offer her more assistance by way of funds and workers, and she'd never be able to repay him.

Neither his kindness nor his money.

"I apologize that our arrangement will last longer than either of us anticipated." In fact, despite her better judgement, Kate hadn't any idea when she'd be able to move back home. "I know it is terribly inconvenient to have me underfoot."

He waved his hand, dispelling her apology. "Do not fret. It is no inconvenience at all. I sent an entreaty to the bank requesting the liquidation of the bank account. At least that will garner enough funds to continue the work needed. I have also called in a favor at Dephino's Lumber outside London. I helped with the proprietor's daughter's dowry agreement, and he is indebted to me—at least by giving us a discount on the materials we will need to complete the work."

Kate noticed how seamlessly Joshua said, "we."

"Why are you being so kind?" Kate blurted. She'd been thinking the question for days but never meant to vocalize it. She understood the importance of helping those less fortunate than yourself. It had been a large part of her parents' mission in Cheapside. Her father counseled those who lived in the area, and her mother attempted to provide affordable education. If Kate were being honest, she didn't want to believe that Joshua had an ulterior motive behind his actions. "I mean…"

Her words trailed off. She was unable to establish any other meaning behind her question.

His eyes narrowed on her. "You are my friend."

Friend? In all her years, Kate hadn't ever called another that. Yes, she'd grown close to some children in her youth, but outside the classroom, they had no association with one another. As they grew older, they moved on, married, and some even moved away from Cheapside. They never reached out to her. There had been young girls and boys she'd met at her father's vicarage, but they too hadn't sought out anything more than their morning of scripture teachings.

The ache she'd suffered after her parents' passing had grown in its depth when not a single person had reached out to give condolences for her loss, besides a few of the men and women of her father's congregation.

"Come now," Joshua said when she remained silent. "You cannot think a friendship between you and me is so out of the realm of possibility. We have much in common. We see each other nearly every day. We wave and greet one another. I handled matters for your father when needed, and for you afterwards. Our respective buildings are across the street from one another."

Besides Mr. Cuttlebottom and mayhap Joshua's uncle, her father had not been a man to keep friends. Neither had her mother outside of sporadic visits from parents of her pupils, and those were never instigated by her mother. Oddly enough, Kate had never given her parents' solidary existence much consideration. "And that makes us friends despite all our—"

"All our what?" Joshua prodded.

"Differences. You are an educated lord, while I am the daughter of an impoverished vicar and a schoolmarm." She pursed her lips, knowing she shouldn't have to spell everything out to him. His upbringing and station as a duke's son should be proof enough. But his blank stare said he at least needed a reminder of where their respective positions in London society stood. "You know as well as I that our paths were never meant to cross, my lord. My life is in Cheapside, it always will be." She swung her arms wide. "And yours is here, in this lovely home, or in your fancy office away from the working-class areas."

"Simply because I was blessed by the circumstances of my birth, you think that means we were never meant to be friends? That friendship between us is out of the question?"

Kate wanted far more than to be simply *friends* with Joshua. She longed to truly belong in his home, in his world. "I am only saying that I believe our friendship is not as normal as most," she said, averting her stare. "My class and your class…your world and my world…could not be more different, no matter what we think of it. Though I relish the notion of our friendship."

"And what if I *believe* I am only able to be who I want to be in your world." He sat forward, his frame no longer relaxed, as if what he planned to share next meant a great deal. And that, in turn, her response was important to him. "What if on the inside, I do not feel like a part of the world I was born into? What if, for that matter, you are meant to be something different, as well? Something more…"

Kate sniffed at his question, wondering what he meant by the statement but also longing for the possibility that what he said could be true. "We are who we are. One cannot change or dispel the circumstances surrounding one's birth. A pauper can never be a prince, just as a prince cannot become a pauper simply because he wishes it so."

"I relent, Miss Kate," he said with a chuckle, reclining once more, though not as comfortably as a few moments before. "However, you mustn't ignore that there is more to life and the paths we take than what is included solely due to our birthright."

Kate desperately wanted to believe in that. She wanted to take his words to heart and live by them, especially since she could not be sure of the circumstances surrounding her birth. For all Kate knew, she was already living above the station she'd been born into. Heavens above, she wanted to defy all her circumstances and proclaim to all that she truly longed for…Joshua.

Clearing her throat, Kate changed the topic before her heart overwhelmed her good sense. "When do you think to hear from the bank?"

He shrugged. "The deposit account was recorded many years ago. It may take time to locate the original paperwork—if it still exists. They may not have the authority to release the funds prematurely and may need to locate the current duke for approval."

"That could take a lot of time." Far more time than they had.

"Yes," Joshua agreed. "Until my men locate Shrewbury, or the bank responds to my request, we keep working. You can continue teaching the children in my office as the repairs progress on your home. And my townhouse is at your disposal for as long as necessary."

"Are you certain I shouldn't sell to Mr. Cuttlebottom?" She'd pondered the possibility the entire previous day, and Joshua would have to admit it was a viable enough option for her. As she summed up the courage to say what needed to be said, she silently hoped he'd speak out against her coming plan. Perhaps admit that he could not think of her no longer living across the street from his office. "With the money, I could purchase a small cottage outside the city or save the funds and apply for a position at one of the many boarding schools around England. I know I am not overly educated, but I am qualified to teach—"

"You cannot think to give up what your parents left to you, even if it sounds easier in the moment."

Kate never wanted to give up what little she possessed—and that had begun to include Joshua as much as her schoolroom and pupils.

"No option is so simple," she retorted. "No matter what is decided, I have much work ahead of me. It does not help that I am at the mercy of others and not in control of what is to come. Plus, I have been forced to accept your generosity, knowing I will never be able to repay you. At least if I sold the building, I would have a small sum to my name."

"And you would leave Cheapside—and the children—behind for a cottage or a teaching position?" His brow rose, and Kate did not feel at ease with him questioning her dedication to her students.

"I hadn't thought the plan through in its entirety. But, yes, if that is where fate took me, it is where I would go." It was unfair and not what she'd choose for her future. However, if given no other alternative, Kate would need to forge a new path. "You, of all people, should understand my need to support myself and not leave my future to chance."

"I do not want you to leave Cheapside." The edge that had entered his tone before was gone, the words leaving on a resigned exhale as whatever had been pent up within him dissipated.

His confession slammed into her as if she'd run into a brick wall. Her head swam, and her stomach began another round of flutters.

He did not want her to leave…

The notion that he truly *did* feel a similar draw to her as she did to him was at once invigorating and terrifying.

"I do not want to leave"—*you*—"Cheapside either. It is my home…the only life I know. But if there is no other option. I would be foolish not to consider it."

Had he not followed a course different than

what his life should have taken? As the son of a duke, he was entitled to live a life free of labor. To spend his days and nights enjoying everything Kate had been denied. Yet, Joshua had taken a different course, a difficult one, and had thrived.

Would he deny her the same opportunity?

"I think it is far too soon to consider such a drastic move, that is all, Kate." Whatever had transpired between them—his confession, her longing, her doubts—fled as quickly as it had come, yet his stare remained locked on her as if she considered fleeing London that same night.

Joshua hastily stood, readying to depart.

Kate longed to ask him to stay…even for just a bit longer.

Being alone with her thoughts was not what she wanted. To be with Joshua, in her private room, discussing any matter of import was what Kate desired. More time for them to be a *we* and not individuals whose paths had crossed by folly. Something more. Their connection fated long before they met.

Joshua had already done so much for her, and all she'd done in return was keep him from his responsibilities: his clients, his work, and his home. Now, he was burdened with her future. She could see it in his eyes.

While it gave Kate some peace to know she had Joshua's backing in whatever decision she made, it was nice to share the weight of it all with him. She was clearly asking too much of him, but she was helpless to avoid it.

This notion of depending on another was new to her. That it was Joshua made the need all the more tempting.

"Sleep well, my lord," she offered, standing. "I shall be ready to depart at our usual time in the morn."

He halted, taking her in from head to toe before glancing into the hearth behind her. The quick move did not stop Kate from noticing the look in his eyes. It was a look she was becoming all too familiar with, though she was not certain what it meant. She could not stop herself from taking a step toward him. His stare darted back to hers when she did.

Reaching out, she took his hand, his skin warm and smooth against hers.

For a brief moment, she pictured her lips on the bare skin of his wrist similarly to how he'd pressed his to her flesh at his office off Bond Street.

His penetrating stare told her he wanted to remain as much as she wished to ask him to stay.

In that moment, the boundaries and differences that separated them evaporated. She was merely a woman…and he a man.

Class, wealth, influence—none of it meant anything.

Kate felt it to her core. She'd always known it. Her father had taught her that when everything was stripped away from a person, the heart was all that was left. It was what loved another, where kindness and compassion originated from, and what would ultimately determine where a person would go in the afterlife.

Joshua was not being awarded anything for assisting her. His offer of friendship came from the purest of intentions. There was no other choice but to believe him—*in* him.

She inhaled sharply. Despite their differences in station, Kate wanted more than friendship.

It was something she'd always longed for—

more than a mere acquaintance.

A confidant. A trusted friend. A person to share her hopes and dreams with.

Someone that could understand that she was more than a teacher, more than a vicar's daughter, more than…

He released her hand, and she felt the connection between them slip away once more.

But she wasn't ready for that. She wasn't prepared to be alone again.

Kate never wanted to return to her solitary life above the schoolroom.

Could it be that Joshua sought more too but was afraid to voice his desires?

She lifted her hand, still warm from his touch, and allowed her finger to graze his cheek. It had been a long day, and she could feel the prickly hairs at his jawline, but that did not deter her. It intrigued her. She wanted to touch more of him, not only his cheek.

"Kate?" His gaze held hers as his hand cupped her face, splaying his fingers against her cheek. "This is…"

"Unseemly and ill-advised?" she whispered.

In response, Joshua stepped forward until there was barely an inch separating them, and a new spark lit his stare. With agonizing slowness, he removed her hand from his cheek, but he did not release it. He placed a kiss on the inside of her wrist again. His warm lips pressed gently into her flesh, so softly Kate did not dare close her eyes, afraid she'd miss the sight and wonder later if it had actually happened or if it were only another of her wayward dreams.

"Nothing about this—or us—is unseemly." He kissed her again, this time on her palm. "If anything, it is untimely as we have been attributing all our attention to your situation and not *our* situation."

"Our situation?" Kate's head swam with the implications, struggling to make sense of everything Joshua was saying. Her feelings—about him, at least—were not new, and they only intensified with his proximity. How had she ever gone about her business across the street from Joshua without realizing her attraction? "The timing?"

"You are a guest in my home, Kate." He sighed. "I have no right to press my company on you or invade your chamber as I have."

"I invited you in." And she was not ready for him to depart.

"Yes, but—" He stepped away, dropping her hand when he did, and paced toward the hearth, pivoting and stalking the room until he halted before the door. "I should go. Please, excuse my impetuous behavior. Until tomorrow."

When he fled the room, he took all the air with him, and Kate strained to breathe in his absence, her chest aching within the constraints of her bodice.

Yes, but…

"Yes, but…what?" She wanted to scream after him.

Kate's mind went over and over the many nights she'd stared down from her window, watching the lights extinguish in his office and waiting to catch a quick glimpse of Joshua before he climbed into his coach and headed off into the invading twilight. She longed to know where he went, what he did, and who he spent the long nights with. Her cheeks blossomed with heat at the many times she'd dreamt of running down the stairs, into the street, and hopping into his coach before it rolled away. There had been so many times she'd caught his eye as he walked across the street and wished to wave him inside her schoolroom. There had been ample time for them to become better acquainted, but neither of them had crossed the invisible line that'd kept them separated without either of them realizing it.

Now, she had answers to at least two of those musings. He came to Cavendish Square, and he remained alone.

As she had each and every night since her parents' passing.

They were more similar than anyone would expect.

And Kate had a feeling Joshua relished being alone about as much as she did…

Which meant, not at all.

CHAPTER 10

ZETA CLUTCHED THE missive in her hand as she took hold of her satchel, stuffed with all her worldly possessions. It had never mattered to her that she had nearly nothing to call her own. Her years with the caravan had been about mutual survival for everyone, not about each individual. But that time was gone now—there was something that belonged to her, and only her.

And it was past time she reclaimed what was hers.

With Lavinia's passing the previous spring, Zeta had nearly given up hope of ever finding Katherina. The harsh winter that'd followed had seen the entire caravan stranded near the Scottish border with few supplies. Thankfully, the snowstorm had passed after a few days, and the high snow drifts had melted with a swiftness Zeta had never witnessed in all her years traveling the land. Since then, they'd spent the year near Westmorland in an area that was more accepting of their vagabond existence.

Zeta had sent a letter to Augusta at Shrewbury, as she often did when she found herself in a town for longer than a fortnight or two. Yet, in the last seven years, she'd never gotten any word back from the maid. Which only meant that nothing had changed. Katherina's whereabouts were still unknown. Zeta refused to believe that it meant anything else. She had to trust that Augusta was still employed at Shrewbury and that she remained focused on locating Katherina.

With blessed relief, Zeta's trust in the woman had finally come to fruition.

A letter had arrived with the afternoon mail coach from Manchester, much to Zeta's utter disbelief. In it was the information she'd been waiting for all these years.

She walked to the far side of the wagon where her horse waited, saddled, and ready to depart. Hefting her satchel up onto the horse's back, she tied the bag tight for her long ride, checking to make sure she'd tucked her provisions inside as well as the spare coins the group had collected for her journey.

Normally, they all traveled together, but there was no time to ready everyone and make the four-day journey by wagon. Time was imperative, and it never failed that a wheel would break, or a horse would go lame. Zeta cared for everyone, but this was her journey to make, and she could not have anything slowing her down. They all understood and supported her decision.

Zeta—no, her name was A'laya, and she needed to get used to it again—took in the gathered men and women around her. Some had been part of the caravan before her, while others joined over the years. Regardless, each and every one held a special place in her heart.

"Ye shall return if ye doona be find'n her?" Charlie asked. The man was young but capable. He'd taken on the task of hunter for the group, and since he'd come to them, they'd never gone without food. "We will wait here for ye 'til the cold hits…then we travel to Liverpool."

Earlier, she'd begged them to do what was best for them, not wait in Westmorland for her return. Because, if what Augusta had written was correct, A'laya would not be returning. The caravan was a fiercely loyal lot, and she'd always appreciated their dedication…but her time with them was at an end, even if Charlie and the others were not immediately accepting of the fact.

The mare stomped her hoof, and A'laya's heartbeat increased, her nervousness matching the beast's anticipation even as her body ached already thinking of the long ride ahead. She'd asked to take the youngest horse for the journey, knowing the broader ones were needed to pull the wagons. The mare had also proven fast with the endurance required to make the trip quickly.

Tucking Augusta's letter into her pocket, A'laya gave hugs all around, knowing that this might very well be the final time she saw any of them. Next, she mounted her mare and looked down the long road ahead of her.

It was late September, and the weather would be warm.

She had enough coin in her satchel to find a room for the night where she could bathe and prepare for the final day's ride into London.

She waved to the caravan and prodded her horse into action as she leaned close to the beast's neck. They flew South to Stuart and Lords, Solicitors, near Bond Street. Augusta had written of a young clerk who'd arrived at Shrewbury seeking the duke. The butler had turned the man away, and he'd started back toward London, but not before Augusta had detained the clerk for a private word.

He'd carried a letter with him, addressed to the Duke of Shrewbury from a Lord Joshua Stuart, Solicitor on behalf of one Miss Katherina Elliott.

Her daughter!

The old duke had spoken the name Elliott all those years ago. She'd been unable to trace a family with the name, but now she knew they were in London, or at least their solicitor was.

The wind whipped at A'laya's hair, and her cheeks grew moist as tears of utter joy slipped down her face to be carried off on the breeze.

This solicitor knew A'laya's daughter, but how well? What could he have been writing the duke about? Had her daughter known of the treachery surrounding her disappearance from A'laya's arms?

There were so many questions. But A'laya felt in her heart that the man held the answers she needed.

The metal between her breasts heated against her skin as if it suspected that A'laya's path of life was finally about to be complete once more.

The lord could be the man responsible for helping Walter and Henrietta hide Katherina from her all these years. But that didn't matter now. The duke and duchess were gone. Pierce, the coward, hadn't been heard from since she spotted him at the pier in Portishead several years prior after she'd heard rumors of his return to England. There was nothing left to hide. No one left to keep A'laya from Katherina.

As she rode, pushing the mare ever faster—harder—she imagined what her precious daughter would look like. Would she recognize her on sight? Did she have A'laya's dark, Barbadian skin tone? Had her eyes remained that greyish-blue from her infancy or had they changed? Had she felt as out of place as A'laya had in the small village she'd grown up in?

It was very likely, especially if the duchess had any part in Katherina's upbringing. It was possible her daughter had never been taught anything of her heritage.

There was time, A'laya reminded herself.

Katherina would only be nineteen—not much older than A'laya had been when she met and wed Pierce.

The surefooted rhythm of her mare's hooves increased A'laya's confidence. This would be the journey—her last one—and she'd finally be reunited with her daughter.

All the many years she'd spent handing out fortunes for a pittance hadn't prepared her for her own fate. She'd passed on hope and sage advice to many but had never truly believed she would one day receive the word she'd been longing for all these years.

Nothing remained in A'laya's way but the distance she needed to travel to London.

Not the duke, not the duchess, not Pierce, and most certainly not Lord Joshua Stuart, Solicitor.

CHAPTER 11

THE AFTERNOON WAS fast nearing twilight when Joshua waved Henry off for the night, pulling his own jacket on as he prepared to collect Kate from across the street. In the nearly two weeks since the fire, they'd settled into a routine. They would travel to Cheapside each morning with the rising of the sun, she'd used his back office to teach lessons, the children would depart at noon, and then Kate worked alongside the men to repair her home. Most days, she forbade Joshua from joining her because, as she declared, she'd inconvenienced him enough by allowing her to stay at his townhouse and teach in his office.

Some days, he listened and did his best to concentrate on his work. Other days, he pushed off most tasks or assigned them to Henry and rolled up his sleeves to help Kate.

And then, each night, they returned to his

townhouse. Together.

Yet, he hadn't invaded her private chambers again. She was basically without a home, and he would not be responsible for pushing her away. They hadn't spoken about their shared moment in her chambers. And he'd needed to remind himself of his duty as a gentleman on several occasions.

Nothing had changed as the days passed, but Joshua became more and more accustomed to having Kate in his life, in his home, and in his office. If she strayed, it was only across the street to her schoolroom. She was always within sight.

Except, she avoided being alone with him outside of their travel and meals.

He'd spent so many years divided from his family, he hadn't realized how much he missed having someone to talk to, to dine with, and to share the day-to-day goings-on. But not simply anyone. At home, he'd always had Dolly close. And at his office, Henry was his constant companion. No, it wasn't just *someone*.

It was Kate.

Companions, work associates, and his grandmother's dear friends, while good people, were not what Joshua needed. He needed Kate…only her.

Before the fire, he remained at his office as late as possible, returning home to find his bed long after dark. But now, he found he needed to occupy himself so as not to declare that they return to Cavendish Square too early. In his home, Joshua had Kate to himself. He needn't share her with the crewmen or Henry or her students.

It was selfish, and Joshua knew it.

In his quest to set himself apart from his lineage, Joshua had only succeeded in isolating himself from his family and the men he'd once considered friends. However, the daily life of a lord did not interest Joshua in the slightest. Men of his age and station were comfortable living off their allowances, wooing women they never intended to wed, and spending their free time at gaming hells.

How many friends had he met at Oxford, only to part ways once they took their places in society?

Certainly, he'd been introduced to many gentlemen of his league as they came to work at Stuart and Lords, but they were not his friends. Despite their equal share partnership, they all viewed him as their employer—as did Henry, Chapman, and his stable hand.

There was Dolly, but Joshua could ask nothing more of his grandmother's aging friend.

As his and Kate's time together lengthened, Joshua found it increasingly difficult to keep himself from wanting to spend more hours of his day with her. He'd known since the moment he made her acquaintance years earlier that she was intelligent and had a kind heart. Though it hadn't been until she lived under his roof that Joshua learned just how caring and compassionate she was. She worried about her schoolroom because she wanted her pupils to learn and go on to live happy, successful lives— not because she would be without a home if it couldn't be repaired.

Her motives were utterly selfless.

When Henry returned from Oxfordshire with the news that Shrewbury Gardens was all but abandoned, Kate had only lowered her head and set about the task of doing as much as she could. Even now, she was across the street removing burnt floorboards alongside the workmen. His savings was dwindling, but Joshua did not care as long as Kate was happy.

He ran his hand through his hair. He'd been foolish enough to believe that luck would be on their side, and the duke would send funds. Unfortunately, in similar fashion to Mr. Caleb Abelston, his solicitor, the Duke of Shrewbury was deceased, and his heir unaccounted for, likely on the Continent, living comfortably while Kate struggled in Cheapside. It irked him that he still had not been able to discover the connection between Kate and the Shrewbury dukedom.

And so, it was as Joshua had always believed—unfair.

He could accomplish nothing more this night; especially laboring over the unjust social classes that kept most of his country's people in near or abject poverty and had Kate believing that their lives were never meant to cross paths. That some invisible force had deemed them unequal.

He could only continue as he was and make do with what he had. That had to be enough…for the time being, at least.

Across the street, two men exited the building, their arms full of their craftsmen tools as they departed for the night. The pair lived deeper in Cheapside in a boarding house for single men. They'd needed work, and Joshua had been obliged to see the work completed by men from the area. He watched as they passed the cobbler's shop and the bookseller's, pausing only briefly as they exchanged a few words with a man standing in the shadows of the walkway before nodding their heads and continuing on as night grew closer.

Joshua extinguished the few candles Henry had left lit for him. While the sun had set behind the row of buildings, it was not so dark yet that it prevented him from collecting his things, locking up, and retrieving Kate for their ride home. With luck, they'd arrive at his townhouse before Dolly retired for the night, and he could thank her for the midday meal she'd packed for Kate and him and tucked away in his carriage without his knowledge.

He smiled. His days were beginning to find a new routine, a better one. However, he was not misguided enough to think that it could be permanent, no matter how much he longed for it to be so. Eventually, the schoolroom would be repaired, and he and Kate would go back to waving at each other from their respective buildings.

She'd made it clear she wanted nothing more; that their stations in life prevented it.

However, he'd seen the longing in her eyes, and it matched his own. Could he prove to her that things did not have to be the way they were?

He moved to the back office and took the key from his desk drawer. The chime sounded in the front.

"I'm collecting my things and will be ready to depart shortly." It was either Chapman, having pulled his carriage around, or Kate, her work for the day complete. His heart raced a bit at the thought of having someone other than his servant to greet him at the end of his day. He dipped to pick up a primer one of the children had discarded on the floor in their haste to leave earlier and returned it to his desk—or, more accurately, *Kate's* desk as she'd been using it during school hours. He headed for the door.

"Lord Joshua Stuart?" an unfamiliar voice asked from the doorway.

"Good evening," he called into the shadows

at the front of the office. Someone stood there, but the darkness obscured them from sight. It was not uncommon for a Cheapside resident to seek him out for legal counsel after they'd finished their workday. "The office is closed for the day. However, I would be happy to schedule an appointment—"

"You are Lord Joshua Stuart…of Stuart and Lords, Solicitors?" the woman prodded.

Joshua took in the sight of the older female, her skirts skimming the floor, the material worn but not tattered. Her hair was piled and pinned atop her head. "Yes." Few people in Cheapside knew about his Bond Street office.

"I am looking for Miss Katherina Elliott." Though her words were a demand, and she stepped farther into the office as she said them, Joshua sensed she did not mean to sound threatening. "You will give me her directions."

Joshua looked over the woman's shoulder. The planks of wood were still nailed into place, covering the gaping holes where the door and front window of Kate's home should be.

"I am sorry, but I cannot—"

"You represent her." The woman's voice deepened with stern conviction and…something else. Something personal. "Where can she be found?"

"Yes, I represent her," Joshua agreed. "She is my client. However, I cannot give you her personal information. How did you find me here?"

"I was originally given the directions to your office off Bond. They sent me here," she paused, clasping her hands before her. "After some prodding, of course. You went to Shrewbury. Was it Pierce who sent you?"

"Pierce De Vere?" This was the first person

he'd come into contact with who seemed familiar with Lord Holderness outside of his less than stellar reputation in town.

"Yes." Agitation flowed off her in heavy waves, and her chin trembled slightly—in an almost familiar way. "Did he send you?"

Joshua shook his head. "No, no. I only know the man by name, and even that, only of late."

"He is not another *client* of yours?"

"Certainly not." The dimness of the room prevented Joshua from seeing the woman's face clearly, but her shifting moods were evident. "I serve only Miss Katherina. I was charged with delivering her stipend on a quarterly basis. Did you come to ask after only De Vere?"

Joshua had given away too much information mentioning the money, but he needed to know what this woman knew before she fled. She stepped from foot to foot in an anxious manner as if she were preparing to flee. If she left his office without sharing what she knew of Kate and De Vere, he might miss the opportunity to truly help Kate.

"I am here for Katherina. Where is she?" The curt, clipped tone had Joshua taking a step back. "I have waited long enough, and I will not wait another moment."

The urgency in the woman's voice had him discarding his jacket and setting about lighting the candles once more. She remained in the doorway, shrouded in shadows from the lack of light within the room, the setting sun outside being of little help.

Light filled the office as he re-lit the wall sconces to reveal the woman. She was dressed as Joshua had suspected in a flowing, multicolored skirt with a thick, jeweled belt and yellowed blouse. The woman pinned him in place with her hardened stare.

It was not that Joshua couldn't move, it was that he didn't *want* to move.

Her hair was shot through with grey, but it did not take much imagination to see it had once been a deep ebony with shining curls. Her swarthy skin had the tone of a thousand desert days but the impact of a thousand frigid nights. Despite all of this, it was her eyes that held him transfixed.

Almond-shaped with a color somewhere between blue and grey as if shortly after birth the color had been held in limbo, refusing to be one or the other yet uniquely both at the same time.

All these years, Joshua had thought the shade one of a kind…something that could not be reproduced in more than one person. The color itself was an impossibility but having another matching set staring at him now was utterly unfathomable.

"Your name, madam?"

The woman's chin notched up several degrees before she spoke. "The Countess of Holderness." She paused, swallowed, and with evident reluctance, added, "A'laya De Vere. Or I once was."

Holderness? Was the name not linked to Shrewbury? And what did she mean, "*I once was*?" There had never been any word that Pierce De Vere had wed, no mention of another in the lineage archives Joshua had scoured, nor in the file they'd found. Nowhere had Joshua found evidence Pierce was living outside of England with a *wife*—and perhaps a family. He was a reprobate, a rakehell, and a gambler.

The woman's name needed verification. Her identity did not.

The resemblance was beyond words and

outside of comprehension. It was more than anything Joshua could have imagined was true.

Why had Kate not told him? Out of everything she'd kept private, why would she choose to keep *this* secret? She'd shared that she'd always felt different—could it be she was unaware of how different she was?

"I am here for my daughter, Lady Katherina De Vere."

The utterance answered every question he'd had since discovering the unknown link between Shrewbury and the Vicar Elliott and his wife. That connection was Kate.

It had always been Kate.

The Elliotts had moved to London when she was but a babe, coming from places unknown, and had purchased a building with a large sum of money. Even in Cheapside, that was a feat, unless—as Joshua and Kate had discovered—a person had been given a bequest of some sort.

"Your hand, my lord." The countess removed her thick, woolen gloves from her hands and held her palms out to him. "Give. Now."

Where had this woman come from, and why was he pleased to see her fierceness?

Joshua was helpless to stop himself from taking the several steps until he stood before the older woman. He should be leery of anyone asserting a claim over Kate. She was his.

No, she wasn't *his*.

But he did as asked. Holding out his hands, she took hold of them and closed her eyes. Her head lowered, and she swayed slightly from side to side before stiffening.

"Can I trust you, my lord?" she mumbled. Though her chin lifted, her eyes remained closed.

She seemed to be listening intently, waiting

patiently for his reply. The brief few moments he'd shared with her had not led him to believe that she was a woman practiced in patience.

"I am unsure," he confessed. "It depends on your intentions concerning Miss Kate."

"Lady Katherina." Her eyes opened, and her penetrating grey-blue stare turned steely as it held his. "My instinct says you can be trusted. You are a protective man, my lord, and I am grateful to learn this. I feared you were somehow involved in keeping Katherina from me."

Involved? Joshua could not be further removed from things.

"My man, Henry, I sent him to Shrewbury," Joshua said, stumbling over his words. He pulled his hands from her grasp and retreated. "Why did you not make yourself known? He brought back word that the duke was not in residence— and hadn't been in some years."

The chime above the door jingled, signaling another had arrived.

"Joshua, I saw the lights extinguished and determined you were ready to depart. I hope I did not keep you waiting." Kate's light voice filled the room. "I must say I accomplished much today, especially if my terribly soiled gown is any indication. The workers informed me that, with a few more days of hard work, we should be ready for the lumber. I've sent word to Sally Ann's elder brother. He's thirteen or so, and strong. He can help some—"

Kate stooped to collect the basket Dolly had packed their noonday meal in, her words cutting off when she finally noticed Joshua wasn't alone.

"Oh, my apologies, my lord." Kate straightened, the basket forgotten as her words returned to a formal nature. "I wasn't aware you were still working. I will go 'round to the stables and wait until you have finished for the day."

Kate—no, Lady Katherina—turned to depart.

"Wait," he and the woman spoke in unison.

His stare locked once more with the elderly woman before him.

"Don't go," he said to Kate. "This concerns you. It is I who should take my leave."

This time, it wasn't only Joshua who froze in place, the woman before him did, as well. Kate's mother. He could not believe the sight before him.

The questions that'd plagued them for the last few weeks were to be answered here and now.

Nearly as an afterthought, Joshua wondered how many questions Kate had kept to herself during all of this.

CHAPTER 12

KATE GLANCED OVER the woman's shoulder at Joshua, attempting to get his attention for a hint of what she'd interrupted and how it could possibly include her. However, his stare was locked on the woman whose back was to Kate. She didn't recognize the voice, nor was she familiar with the woman's chosen style of dress. Her skirts were a rainbow of colors that Kate suspected were difficult to obtain, even with an extensive collection of the best dyes available at the local market. She did not recognize her as a woman from the neighborhood nor a shop owner in Cheapside.

"No, my lord, there is no need for you to leave." The woman's icy tone was more than a warning. It was a threat. But what threat could this stranger pose to Kate? "This matter is as much about you as anyone else."

The bank would not have sent a woman to

convey official business, and she was far too advanced in age to be a courier. The hour was growing late, and the day was fast approaching night. The businesses in Cheapside—and Kate assumed all over London—had closed for the evening hours.

"Miss Kate." Joshua cleared his throat, finally glancing past the woman to Kate. "May I introduce the Countess of Holderness, Lady A'laya De Vere."

"But Henry was told..." Kate fell silent as the woman turned to face her. Everything about her was familiar in a way the vicar and his wife had never been. Kate's jawline, her rich skin tone, and her almond-shaped eyes were mirrored in the woman's countenance. Not to mention she was precisely the same height as Kate, and their hair held a similar curl. "...the duchess had passed away, and there was only mention of the earl. Never a wife."

Her last words were spoken barely above a whisper as Kate's stare held the woman's face— so similar to Kate's own.

The haphazard lady looked nothing like any countess Kate had ever imagined. Her hair was long and knotted as if it hadn't seen a proper washing in weeks. Her blouse was yellowed and wrinkled, dusty from travel. Even her shoulders were slouched.

But her eyes were sharp—and a very familiar hue.

"My lady." Kate dipped into a clumsy curtsey. "It is a pleasure to make your acquaintance."

Behind her, she heard the jingle of reins as Joshua's carriage pulled to the curb outside the office, ready to take them back to Cavendish Square. Neither Kate nor the countess moved.

Something within her felt complete, while another part of her, debatably a more significant piece, splintered and shattered into a million bits.

The chime echoed in the quiet room as Joshua's driver pushed open the door. "Ready, my lord?"

"Can you give us a few moments?" Joshua asked the driver before gesturing toward the back room Kate had used for nearly two weeks. "I think we should retire to my office to speak privately. We shan't be interrupted there."

When neither woman moved, Joshua nodded to Kate, who slipped by the countess and him and walked quickly toward the rear of the building. Her steps were stilted, the confusion in her mind making her body work extra hard to move.

She didn't give a whit about privacy. She needed to know why her likeness was reflected in the countess's face. How it was possible? And…and…and…

Kate was uncertain where to begin to try and understand what was transpiring around her. *To* her. She'd never heard of Shrewbury before the fire. Or the De Vere family name. Her parents had never spoken of living in Oxfordshire. And while Kate had held her doubts about who had given birth to her, she'd never imagined she was related to a countess.

Behind her, the elderly woman's footfalls were slow and light, while Joshua's were as they always were, assured and steady. It gave Kate confidence despite how jumbled her thoughts were. Joshua was here, by her side, and together, they would sort it all out.

"May I ask what is going on?" Kate pivoted to face the pair who'd entered the office after her, with Joshua hurrying to light the candles in the room. Even in the darkness, the truth of the situation could not be hidden. "My lady, I cannot deny that I see an uncanny resemblance between you and I. Am I correct to assume we are related?"

"More than that, Kate," Joshua breathed.

"Far more," the woman concurred.

"Can we please start from the beginning?" Kate asked.

Joshua gestured to the row of seats she'd set up for her pupils. "Let us sit, please."

The countess glanced sideways at Joshua but did as requested, selecting a tall-backed, wooden chair. Kate sank into the open seat next to her, while Joshua moved behind his desk. Despite being overwhelmed, Kate was drawn to sit near the woman, to feel her presence as if the nearness would be enough to sort out everything in her mind and return the clarity Kate had felt before entering Joshua's office.

"You have been receiving funds?" It was the countess who broke the silence first. "All these years…"

"My uncle was charged with delivering a quarterly stipend to Vicar Elliott and his wife before they passed. After that, the money arrived on schedule but addressed to Miss Katherina Elliott, their daughter." Joshua folded his hands on his desk, but Kate could feel his discomfort as he stumbled over the word *daughter*. "I continued in my uncle's stead until a few weeks ago when a fire ravaged Kate's building and money was needed for repairs."

This was Kate's mess to handle, not Joshua's. But his presence gave Kate the courage to speak up.

"We learned then a bank had been issuing the funds from an account set up nearly twenty years ago with an initial bequest of ten thousand pounds for the purchase of the building across the street." It seemed odd that it was necessary to explain any of this to the woman as it was *her* family who'd been responsible for it all.

"Around the time you were taken from me," the countess whispered. Tears appeared in her eyes, and Kate had the overwhelming urge to pull the woman close and embrace her.

At the same time, Kate was confused. Taken from her? Perhaps it was only Kate who didn't understand.

Joshua cleared his throat, seemingly unsurprised by the countess's claim.

"My lord?" She willed Joshua to tell her everything he knew. Besides her doubts regarding the vicar and his wife, her *parents*, Kate hadn't been ready to disparage their memory by voicing her concerns surrounding their past and her origins. "Please, tell me all you know."

"Kate, the countess believes you are her daughter." He glanced at the older woman sitting beside Kate. "Lady Katherina De Vere."

"That cannot be right. I am Miss Katherina Elliott." She'd always felt there was something not quite right about her mother and father. However, they'd loved her, they'd cared for her, and they'd made certain she was taken care of after their passing—as best they could anyway. She'd lived a pious life, but she'd never wanted for anything. She'd noticed their differences, of course, but admitting aloud to a stranger what she'd suspected her entire life was too much. A betrayal to the mother and father who'd raised her. "My father was a vicar, and my mother dedicated her life to educating those less fortunate. That is who I am. Miss Katherina Elliott of Cheapside."

It was who she'd been raised to be. A lowly vicar's daughter. A woman resigned to her place in life. Blessed and fortunate for what she possessed as others survived on far less.

Not the daughter of an earl and a countess.

And certainly, far from the granddaughter of a duke and duchess.

The Countess of Holderness looked on stoically, issuing no challenge, only listening until Kate was finished.

"My name is A'laya. I was wed to Pierce De Vere, only son of the Duke and Duchess of Shrewbury. At the time, he was Earl of Holderness, and I, the countess." She spoke with a sure, steady voice, never once faltering. "Believing us in love, I agreed to move with him to his family's home at Shrewbury Gardens, where I gave birth to a beautiful baby girl. When she was—when *you* were—two months old, the duchess, Pierce's mother, ripped you from my arms, and you disappeared. Not long after, I was sent away, almost literally dumped alongside the road and left to die in the harsh elements."

Kate turned to Joshua. If the woman were lying, he would know—or he would know someone who held the truth. However, he only nodded at her, confirming the countess's claims.

"This is true?" Kate asked. "How can it be so?"

"I have searched for you since you were taken." The countess—her *mother*?—stared hard at her. "Tell me you were treated kindly all these years."

"My mother and father"—both Kate and the lady flinched at her word choice—"the vicar and his wife, loved me greatly. Unconditionally."

"And you have lived here all your life?"

Kate pointed toward the front of the

building, though at some point, Joshua had closed his office door, making it impossible to see through the room and out the front window. "I was raised above the schoolroom across the street. My father's vicarage was only a block away. I learned in the schoolroom alongside the other children."

"The duke and duchess...you never knew them?"

Kate shook her head. "It was only us, my mother and father and I. Except for Joshua and his uncle."

"That is a blessed miracle." A bit of the tension eased from the woman's wrinkled, weathered face. She appeared years younger than she had only a moment before. "The duchess, Henrietta De Vere, was a vile, despicable woman. I prayed every day that you would remain far from her, even if that meant you were far from me, as well."

The countess was speaking of people Kate didn't know and had no connection to. However, her mother, A'laya, sat before her. "Where have you been all these years?"

"Searching for you, Katherina." She placed her palm to Kate's cheek and smiled. Kate could not help but nestle into her hand, breathing deeply of a new scent. That of her mother. "I never gave up hope that I would find you. I've lived with a traveling group—mystics and fortune tellers—and we've journeyed all across England and Scotland. In every village, in every town, I asked after you."

"And my father, Pierce De Vere, he let this happen? He allowed me to be taken and given away. And the vicar...I cannot believe he would have been part of such a ruse." She could not believe the man she'd known as her father for her entire life would have allowed such a travesty to occur. That he would participate in keeping a babe from its mother. Were they unaware of where Kate had come from? Maybe they didn't know her past and had simply taken in a child who needed a home. They'd been good people, kind, revered by those in Cheapside and known for helping others. "No, it is worse than that, isn't it? My *true* father paid someone to take me."

The countess lowered her head as tears fell down her face, then dripped off her chin to land on her many-hued skirts. The moisture dampened the fabric and brightened the colors.

Tears were not enough to repair the destruction done by the woman's revelations.

Kate was not who she believed herself to be. Her parents were likely not who they'd purported themselves to be. The schoolroom was her home, but it had been purchased with ill-gotten funds, and Kate knew she could never think the same of the place she'd considered her home. And now, a stranger claimed that everything she'd ever known was a falsehood. She'd been lied to all her life. What was Kate to do with all this knowledge?

She'd longed for answers for so long, even before she knew there were answers to find. What she'd never expected was to discover something that could destroy what little she had left in her life.

CHAPTER 13

A'LAYA FINALLY HAD her Katherina next to her; she could smell the scent of her skin, hear the lilt of her voice, and see the resemblance they shared. And she could barely bring herself to meet her daughter's stare as the tears flowed warm and unabated down her face. She'd dreamt of this moment for nearly two decades, and now words eluded her. All the things she'd labored over every day and night, all the people she'd cursed with every breath, and the immense, hollow, gaping hole within her still gnawed at her.

She'd played no hand in Katherina being taken from her, yet A'laya could not cast off the shroud of guilt she felt regarding her part in it all. She'd been young and naïve. She'd allowed herself to believe that anything was possible with love. She'd given trust when it hadn't been earned nor warranted.

And Katherina had paid the ultimate price.

Living every moment knowing her daughter was out there somewhere but having no notion where and with whom, had been a horrid way to live. But what would come next? Katherina had lived a normal life with two loving parents, a home, and a future, only to have it stripped from her by a stranger. She would question everything in her life thus far: her childhood, the people she'd thought family, and even her own identity.

Yet again, A'laya was to blame.

A'laya had had years to come to terms with what Pierce and his family had put her through, forced upon her, and how they'd discarded her.

Katherina did not know the entirety of it all. She only knew that her life was being torn asunder.

Was it selfish for A'laya to come into her daughter's life after all these years?

Perhaps Katherina would have fared better had A'laya not searched for her.

She lifted her head and brushed the tears from her cheeks.

She would not think in such a way. Could not think in such a manner. She needed Katherina. And no matter how it all hurt in that moment, her daughter needed her, too.

There was so much she longed to share with Katherina, and even more that A'laya desired to learn about the daughter who'd grown up without her. When had she taken her first steps? What had been her first word? Did she excel at learning? Had she many friends? Did she prefer summer over winter? Even the simplest question, Katherina's favorite color, was unknown to A'laya.

"My lady." The soft tone of Lord Joshua Stuart's voice was unexpected. "With your agreement, I think we should return to my townhouse. Kate—Katherina—has been residing there since the fire. I have plenty of room, and I am certain we are all famished. My carriage is just outside."

A'laya had arrived in London expecting to face a foe in the solicitor, yet she'd found him to be kind and, most of all, trustworthy. An ally. Lavinia had taught her years before that reading someone wasn't about mystic powers as much as it was about intuition. A'laya could confess that she'd been severely lacking in instinct. With Lavinia's tutelage and support, she'd learned the skill with a swiftness the older woman had claimed was uncommon and a rarity.

When she'd held the lord's hand earlier, he hadn't tensed, nor had his palm moistened with nerves. He'd looked her in the eyes, and his stare hadn't wavered even an inch. His breathing did not quicken nor halt. He hadn't bestowed a false smile on her nor evaded her questions, except when it came to withholding information that would protect Katherina.

She hadn't known a more honorable peer since her father's passing.

A'laya suspected that if he thought she would cause Katherina any harm, the lord would not have allowed her to get within sight of her daughter.

"I appreciate your offer and desperately wish for more time with Katherina," A'laya said, accepting the man's kindness. "I shall follow on my mare."

"It is late, and the temperature is falling rapidly." He shook his head as he stood. "You will ride in the carriage with us."

She caught Katherina studying her, taking in her attire and her hair. She should have spent the extra coin to bathe at the inn the previous night, but A'laya hadn't known what she'd discover when she arrived in London, and she had only enough coin for one more stay at an inn.

"I think it best I follow on horseback, my lord." She'd come to speak with the solicitor. She hadn't dreamt she'd find Katherina so quickly. The situation was moving far faster than A'laya had expected, and a few moments to think everything through would be beneficial for both of them. "I will ride behind you the entire way."

"Night is upon us, and I fear this is when thieves and other miscreants frequent the streets of London." Katherina stood and stared down at her, her eyes softening. "It is not safe."

"I can care for myself." Never, not since being dumped on the side of the road, had A'laya allowed herself to be helpless in any situation. "The offer of a bed and a hot meal are generous enough."

And the opportunity to spend more time with Katherina. It was more than she'd hoped to gain on her journey to London.

"It is settled." Lord Joshua Stuart clasped his hands and gave both women a tentative smile. "Katherina and I will ride in the carriage, and the countess will follow on her own horse. Shall we be off?"

A'laya's knees and back ached as she stood. She shook out her skirts and nodded.

She should be overwhelmed with the idea of seeing her daughter after all these years; however, finding her was only the beginning. There was so much they needed to discuss— mostly that A'laya never would have consented to giving her babe away. Nor would she have abandoned her... not for anything or anyone.

As they departed the building, she was

struck by how much Katherina resembled A'laya's own mother. Her coloring was several shades lighter, but her upturned nose, her rounded chin, her long, curling, ebony hair were all things inherited from her Barbadian lineage. In addition to the likeness, Katherina had her grandmother's kind heart but without A'laya's ingenuousness. The woman was capable and independent. She possessed a cultured tone despite being raised away from a noble family. She seemed skilled at knowing who to trust, as evidenced by Lord Joshua's presence in her life.

Katherina had survived without A'laya. She'd done more than survive, she'd thrived.

All while A'laya had been slowly dying on the inside.

"Please ride close to the carriage, my lady," Lord Joshua warned as he offered to assist her onto her horse. "Chapman will keep watch. The distance is not overly far."

Katherina stood in the shadows near the carriage, holding a basket A'laya hadn't seen her collect.

"She will listen. I promise," he whispered in A'laya's ear. "Kate—she is known as Miss Kate to everyone in Cheapside—has encountered much change and uncertainty of late. However, she is always understanding, even with those undeserving of her time. Though I pray that is not the case here."

Atop her mare, A'laya kept a close watch as the solicitor returned to the carriage and assisted her daughter inside.

A'laya also prayed she was deserving of Katherina's understanding and kindness.

She prodded her mare into a slow trot and fell in line beside the conveyance. The crisp London night air bit at her face and instantly chilled the tears that began falling once more.

There was much A'laya had to be thankful for as she kept pace through the darkened streets: finding her daughter in good health, the compassion of the solicitor, and the hope that A'laya had held onto every day, even when it threatened to abandon her in hard times.

Mostly, A'laya was thankful the turn of the carriage wheels and the clopping of the horse's hooves masked the gut-wrenching sobs that erupted from her without restraint.

CHAPTER 14

KATE SAT ACROSS from Joshua in the carriage, desperately trying to suppress the urge to pull the drapes aside and press her face to the foggy glass to keep watch on the woman who trailed them on horseback. She succeeded and forced her hands to remain in her lap, though tightly winding and unwinding the fabric of her skirts, crushing the material until it was beyond wrinkled. This woman, this *stranger*, held all the secrets…answers to things Kate hadn't known to look for. She could not risk having her questions go unanswered for even one more day.

The possibility that the countess—her mother—would disappear into the night as quickly as she'd appeared was nearly as frightening as accepting everything the woman claimed to be true. Why should it matter that some lord she'd never heard of before the fire and his parents had sent her away? The vicar and his wife, the two people Kate adored above all else, had loved her in return. They'd raised her in a safe home and encouraged her to be a kind and caring person. Yet they'd hidden a momentous and life-altering truth from her all these years. Had it weighed heavily on them? If they were still with her, would they be remorseful? Would they have broken down and insisted that she find her true family?

Had the secret slowly crushed her parents over the years as Kate grew up? Did they sense that Kate never truly belonged with them or in Cheapside? And if the countess hadn't found her this night, would Kate have ever discovered the truth of her past?

Everything should be far simpler than it was. Kate had believed herself alone in the world only that morning. Now, she'd discovered that she had a mother and possibly more family. She wasn't alone. Nor was she plain Miss Kate. She was Lady Katherina De Vere. If she could not find the funds to fix the schoolroom, it would not mean that she'd be left without a home or would be dependent on Joshua's charity with no plans for her future. The news she'd just received changed everything. Not how she felt about others, but how she felt and accepted herself. For so long, she'd built this wall between herself and those around her, especially with Joshua. But as her mother had spoken, that barrier had crumbled, exposing all of Kate's misconceptions about her past, her present, and all the stark possibilities her future now held.

She had a mother...family, even if it only turned out to be the two of them. From the haphazard appearance of the countess, Kate doubted she had much more to her name than Kate herself did. Though, as the vicar—Kate's mind halted—no, he was still her father despite their lack of shared blood. Her father had always told her that possessions did not make the man, nor could one be fulfilled and whole simply because they possessed a grand house, servants, and coffers of money.

Pain sliced into her palm, and Kate looked down to see her fists clenched so tightly that her nails had bitten through her gloves and into the soft skin beneath.

"Kate?" Joshua took hold of her hands and leaned so close she could smell his spiced scent. This man, someone who had been no more than a neighbor and acquaintance not long ago, had turned into her only constant. He helped but asked nothing of her. He listened but never dictated what she should do. He'd had the foresight and ingenious idea to seek out Shrewbury and the bank who held her account, but he'd never forced any decisions upon her. He always knew what to do, where to go, and whom to trust. All while Kate seemed continually on the verge of falling apart…helpless and despondent.

Looking up from their clasped hands, Kate met his brown stare. The resolute persona she'd managed since meeting the countess crumbled. She'd felt it happening on the inside but only now, with Joshua close, did she let it show outwardly. If she were a spool of thread, she'd surely be unraveling, winding across the ground, never knowing when it would all come to an end or where she'd end up when it did.

"When you offered to help me, I imagine you did not expect for all this…trouble." She sighed on the last word, unable to pull a better term from her addled haze. "The workmen said the upper floor of the schoolhouse is suitable for living again while the repairs are made. I think it best if I return—"

Joshua had his own life to live. His attention was better focused on his businesses and his clients, not her. She'd brought messiness into his neatly organized life. And it appeared that things would likely spin even more out of control before Kate could get a firm grasp on everything.

He shook his head as he slipped from the seat across from her in the moving carriage to kneel on the floor between them, his body swaying gently from the conveyance rocking to and fro. "I cannot let you go. Not now...with everything."

"I belong in Cheapside, Joshua," Kate countered. It was the same conversation they'd had several times since the fire. "My home is there, I was raised there, and the children need me. It does not matter that the circumstances of my birth have changed."

She'd expected him to refute her justifications. They were the same things she'd used to prove that they could not share anything beyond an acquaintance of friendship. He was the child of a duke, which he could not change. Yet, now she'd learned that she'd been born nobility, as well. His childhood and noble birth proved he did not belong in Cheapside, while her upbringing, despite her noble origins, trapped her to a life in Cheapside.

She was a hypocrite, and she waited for him to accuse her of it.

"I think the countess needs you more than anyone in Cheapside." He twined their fingers until they were laced securely together and then squeezed gently. "And, no matter how independent you are, you need her, too."

What Kate needed was for Joshua to guide

her, to tell her how to fix everything without banishing the few remaining beliefs she had about her past and where her future lay. She longed for him to assure her that everything would be all right. They'd return to his townhouse, find their respective beds for a long night of rest, and in the morning, they'd both awaken to find it had all been a cruel dream—wayward and sinful as it was. How many times had the vicar warned her about longing for a life above her station? How many times had her mother showed her that a pious existence helping others was fulfilling and more than some could ever hope for? Kate should be grateful and not allow her mind to stray to a future anywhere but in her schoolroom. Alone.

The appearance of Lady De Vere and her harrowing tale of being cast out and abandoned changed nothing. Kate was still near penniless with little more than a damaged building to her name. She should be grateful for how blessed she was to possess what she did when others, many of them her pupils' families, had so much less.

The folly of her fortune in life had never been so startlingly laid bare before her as it was now.

None of what the countess had said should matter, but it did. She'd lived her life allowing others to keep her in the dark—her parents, and to a certain extent, Joshua—all while deluding herself into believing that she had a firm grasp on her life. She'd believed herself independent because she contained herself in a bubble of sorts. Kate had lived without letting anyone in, without allowing anyone to truly know her. In turn, she hadn't really gotten to know anyone else either. That needed to change. It must, or Kate would have nothing left when the money ran dry. She'd be unable to feed herself, let alone help the children of Cheapside.

And she'd suffer alone.

She had little choice but to embrace who she was in all its nuances and explore her past—or risk losing everything.

Her vision clouded as tears pooled in her eyes at the same time a new, raw clarity settled around her. "What I need, what I've always needed, is the truth—no matter how hurtful it is. My parents died without telling me anything of my past…of *their* past. If they lied to me about so many things, it is possible Mr. Cuttlebottom speaks the truth about the building, and my father did agree to sell my home to him. Who is this woman, the countess? And where did she come from? Why was I unwanted—something to be kept hidden and eventually forgotten? And why all the secrecy behind the bequeathal to the vicar?"

She fell silent as her questions continued echoing in her mind. *Who* was she, and what did all of this mean for her future?

Forgetting everything would be impossible. Continuing as she had before today would be foolish, as well. And accepting her new identity, while heartbreaking and terrifying at the same time, might be a necessity.

"You are confused," Joshua whispered. "And rightly so, I fear."

"What do I do, Joshua?" She pulled her hands from his and brushed away a tear before it blazed a path down her cheek to betray her fragile state. She'd attempted to handle matters herself, but it had become more and more apparent that Kate needed Joshua. "You've guided me of late. You must know what I should do next and what is to come. Do I listen to the woman and forsake my parents, tarnishing their memory? Or should I refuse to listen, cast the woman out, and attempt to forget everything?"

"There is no easy path or simple answer." He pressed his fingers to her jaw, lifting her chin. "However, I do know that nothing you learn today can alter who you are. You are still Katherina...sweet, caring, and intelligent. You are a daughter, a friend, and a teacher. None of that has changed. Anything new we learn about your past will only add to what you already are, not take away from it. This is a decision— whatever it is—that you must make for yourself and no one else."

Kate wished his words were true, longed for him to be correct because if he were, they'd one day be able to return to how things were before the fire. Before she'd moved into his townhouse, and before Lady De Vere appeared in his office. They'd once more be solicitor and teacher.

He could remain in her life and she in his.

She'd lied when she claimed they couldn't be friends.

Kate longed to call Joshua her friend, though she desired to be more to him. Her heart longed for him in a completely different manner. To go back to the days when she watched him leave his office at sunset from her bedchamber window and dreamt of where he went at night before she knew of his grand house. Back to the days he'd saunter into her schoolroom with a friendly, bright smile and a hearty joke for the children. Back to the times when she'd wave as she and the children marched down the street toward the bookseller.

In that alternate reality, Kate could hold fast to him and not ponder the possibility of him leaving her life. She didn't need to fret over what she would do or where she'd go once her trust was completely depleted. In those days, before she'd discovered that her body, her mind, and her *very soul* craved him, she hadn't had to confront the many troubling aspects of her life. Not her suspicions surrounding the vicar and his wife or the holes concerning her heritage. She'd been able to love them as her parents—nothing more and nothing less.

However, if she entertained a conversation with the countess, everything could—and likely would—change. Accepting her new place as the daughter of nobility might well mean her existence in Cheapside could not continue as it had, even if she attempted to keep everything the same.

CHAPTER 15

THE TWO WOMEN—one he'd known for years, and another he'd only just met that day—sat side by side, neither truly seeing what Joshua saw before him. Beyond their distinct appearances, their posture was similar, each tucking one ankle behind the other, hands clasped in their laps. They made a striking pair. Even their voices were of the same light melody he'd come to relish hearing when Kate spoke.

He imagined how the pair would have taken London society by storm to enchant every lord and gain the envy of most ladies.

Kate…the daughter of a countess.

The news changed nothing about how Joshua felt for Kate. She was still the intelligent, compassionate, giving woman he'd known since journeying to Cheapside all those years ago. Be her nobility or a gentlewoman, Joshua did not care. His heart knew not the difference—and his mind agreed. He was not fool enough to think it didn't matter to those of the peerage, but to Joshua, it was insignificant.

Her strength had not wavered, even when faced by such life-altering information. If anything, her beauty had multiplied in his eyes. She was not resigned to wear a façade, portraying one thing on the outside while being different on the inside.

Though she hadn't known who she was or what her past held, Kate had always had a true sense of who she wanted to be.

The trio had retired to Joshua's mother's favored sitting room immediately upon arriving at Cavendish Square. Joshua had bid a maid to collect Dolly and send her to join them before setting about bringing tea to the sitting room.

Dolly, ever the perfect lady's companion, had entered the room and hardly showed any shock at the older woman's presence. She hadn't batted an eye when A'laya had been introduced as the Countess of Holderness, though she preferred simply A'laya. Nor had she so much as flinched when she was told that A'laya was Kate's mother.

There was nothing Joshua could do as introductions were completed, tea was served, and the room fell silent.

Both Kate and the countess picked at the stitching in their skirts.

It was as if they both dreaded the conversation that was to come, except Joshua could see no reason for either woman to be fearful.

"Tell me, my lady," Dolly said, setting her cup on the table at her elbow. "I have always admired Miss Kate's complexion. It is not the sickly pale that most young women favor of late.

I am pleased to note that she gained it from you."

Joshua held his breath but was relieved when the countess smiled.

"Many years ago, my grandmother, Zeta, met a man in Barbados when his ship, the *Bonnie Belle*, docked near her home." A'laya paused for a moment, but when Kate seemed to lean closer, taken in by news of her past, the woman continued. "His name was Samson. They fell in love, and she sailed back with him to England. They wed shortly after and started their family."

"That is very intriguing." Dolly sighed, pressing her palm to her chest. "Please, do go on…"

Joshua noticed that Kate had stopped fussing with her gown, though her fingers trembled.

He set his hand on hers and squeezed gently. He could not begin to fathom how it felt to have a person walk into your life and tell you that everything you knew about yourself was wrong. That everything you'd grown up believing was not the truth. That every person you loved had kept secrets from you.

Glancing at Kate, Joshua saw her nod to the countess, her gaze transfixed on the woman.

"When they returned to England, my grandfather took a position as a steward with Baron Oderton. Years later, my mother fell in love with the baron's son, my father, Eugene Banesworth."

"What a marvelous tale." Dolly turned to Kate, her grin mischievous and one Joshua knew well. "Can you imagine, Miss Kate? Oh, true love is a blessed thing, is it not, Joshua?"

His late grandmother's companion had never been known for her subtlety when she took a notion to heart.

"It is," Joshua muttered.

"And what of you, my lady?" Dolly continued, smiling in A'laya's direction. "Have you ever wed? From the looks of Kate, her father was a dashingly handsome man, indeed."

Joshua silently chastised himself for not having a word with Dolly before she entered the room. He'd only wanted the countess to know that Kate had not been residing under his roof without a proper chaperone.

A'laya stared down into her tea, steam still rising from the untouched cup. "I did, though I cannot confess it was a marriage based on love."

Joshua winced, knowing some of what was to come.

"The Earl of Holderness was a dashingly handsome lord, but he was not a kind man, nor an attentive husband."

"We certainly know a few of those types, don't we, Joshua?" Dolly's mouth pinched in a tight frown, and she shook her head. "I have known a few rascals in my day, I can assure you, my lady."

A'laya looked up at her daughter, and Joshua would have been a fool not to notice the look that passed between the pair. If he were a betting man, he would guess that it was the first of many the newly acquainted women would share in the days—and years—to come.

"I wed young, and my naiveté was to my detriment—and Katherina's." The countess brought her cup to her lips and took a short, tentative sip before lowering the tea once more. It was only after a deep breath that she spoke again. "Before long, I was with child, and my husband had abandoned me at his family's home in Oxfordshire. It took many, *many* years before I even so much as laid eyes on the man again."

"You've seen him?" Tension had Kate sitting

up straight as if a rod had been placed in her spine. "When?"

A'laya's eyes narrowed, and Joshua sensed the woman's unease for the first time. "It was only a few years ago. He arrived by ship, and I got the barest glimpse of him. But you were not with him, and so, he mattered naught to me."

Dolly had fallen silent, never one to revel in the misfortunes of others.

"Did you know anything about your father's or his mother's duplicity or of the time when she took you from me?" A'laya's question was barely a whisper. "What have you been told?"

"Nothing." Kate's voice was resolute. "While I always sensed I was different, I was never told that the vicar and his wife were not my true parents—though they loved me as if I were theirs."

The conviction in Kate's words must have given the countess pause because she did not immediately speak again.

They'd spoken of A'laya's past—what she knew, where she'd been, and everything she'd lived through, but they'd not talked about Kate. She hadn't been cursed with the same fate as her mother. Kate had been loved and well cared for.

"I feared as much, though I must admit I am relieved to know you had a proper upbringing, even if I was not there for you."

"It was not your fault," Kate said, holding her mother's stare for several seconds before looking away.

Joshua wondered where they all went from here as he took in Kate, the countess, and Dolly. They were a motley group with far more in common than most.

So much needless hurt between them. So many lost years. There was no way to gain any of it back, and he was reasonably sure they'd never know the reasoning behind all of it. Why had A'laya's husband abandoned her? Why had the duchess taken Kate from her mother and sent her away? And where was Pierce De Vere when it all happened?

Joshua had known Kate for years—even though several of those had been in the capacity of mere acquaintances—yet he could not envision his life or his future without her as a part of it.

Joshua couldn't walk away.

Bloody hell, he couldn't imagine a morning without her nestled in the carriage with him as they sped across London to Cheapside.

He was utterly in love with her.

With each day, with each new challenge, Joshua needed her more.

He'd fooled himself into believing his work in Cheapside enabled him to discover who he was and what he wanted for his future. That wasn't true at all. Because Joshua wouldn't be himself without Kate.

Suddenly, he realized they could be anywhere—Cheapside, Bond Street, even on the open ocean in a rowboat. As long as she was by his side, Joshua would know his course.

"Mayhap I should show the countess to her bedchamber for the evening." Dolly pushed to her feet, somehow sensing they all needed time to think, arrange their thoughts, and begin the conversation anew later. "I've had the peach chamber prepared. It is next to Miss Kate's and has a lovely view of the gardens."

When Joshua and A'laya stood, Kate rose, as well, smoothing her palms down her skirts.

She paused for only a second before crossing the scant few feet separating her and the countess and wrapping her arms around her mother. The two women remained in their embrace for several moments, and he noticed that they whispered into each other's ears before Kate squeezed one last time and stepped back.

A'laya smiled warmly, bid Joshua a good evening, and told Kate she looked forward to seeing her in the morning.

Joshua wanted to push Kate to go with her mother, but the selfish part of him longed for her to stay with him. He didn't say a word when the two women, Dolly in the lead, departed the room, leaving the door open in their wake.

Joshua observed Kate watching them bustle from the room, her shoulders stiff, and her breathing shallow.

KATE DREW IN a deep breath the moment Dolly and the countess exited the room. Once again, she was astounded by the fact that everything could change while remaining unchanged at the same time.

She had a mother, yet she'd always had one—an adoptive mother.

She had a past, a heritage, generations of family—and though she hadn't known of her heritage, it did not alter her memories of her childhood, it only enhanced them.

So much came into focus the more her mother shared about her past—*their* past. She wanted to know everything, craved an understanding of who she was and where she'd come from. Even learning of the earl's duplicity where A'laya was concerned did not stave off her need for more details.

Barbados?

As the countess had spoken, Kate had searched her memory for the nation's location.

If she remembered correctly, it was a smallish isle along the shipping routes of the many trading companies' vessels that traveled to places far removed from England.

"My lord?"

Kate focused on the doorway her mother had departed through to where a servant stood, a parcel in his hands.

"Evans." Joshua nodded. "Good evening."

"Gregory from your office delivered this a few moments ago." His stare settled on Kate for a brief moment before moving back to Joshua. "He said it arrived after everyone had departed."

Joshua took the large envelope and turned it over in his hands.

Kate sank back onto the lounge where she'd sat before, stock-still while her mother had spoken so openly to all of them, relaying tales of her tragic past. She would never forget the feel of the older woman in her arms when Kate had embraced her. She'd been rigid as if she hadn't expected the hug. Kate honestly hadn't realized her course of action until her arms were around her mother, and the new scent of the countess embedded itself in Kate's memory. She smelled of open air and…wild flowers mixed with leather, likely from her long ride to London.

The scents were new to her because Kate hadn't traveled outside of London in all the time she'd lived there. The pungent smell of the crowded London streets and burning coal was as common to Kate as the scent of an old book, its paper tainted by years of handling.

"Kate?" The concern in Joshua's tone cut through the fog surrounding Kate and her thoughts. "Kate, are you unwell?"

"My apologies." She leapt to her feet, surprised that while her head swam and felt weighed down by a dense haze, her body was quick to action. "I should leave you"—her eyes flitted to the open parcel in his hands—"to your work."

His brows drew low. "The parcel is for you. Well, it was addressed to me, but the letter inside is for you."

"For me?" She glanced past Joshua, but the servant had departed the room, closing the door behind him. Joshua held out the letter, but Kate could not bring herself to take it. "Are you certain?"

"It arrived from the bank. And, yes, it is addressed to you."

She stared at the missive and then up at Joshua. He nodded, giving her the courage to take it.

There was nothing she could learn that could shock her more than discovering the countess's existence.

Finally, Kate grasped the envelope and read the erratic script on the outside. It was faded and nearly illegible, but Kate could make out her name.

She slipped her finger under the wax seal and removed the letter.

The same hurried script covered the page from edge to edge as if its writer had needed to fill every available inch with words to be shared.

Katherina,

If you are receiving this missive, you have either reached a certain age, and your bequest has run dry, or you've figured out far more than was expected. Either way, the Bank of England has not been foolish enough to go against my wishes. I may be old, but I am still a duke. This letter is to inform you, Miss Katherina Elliott, that a new account with the Bank of England can be accessed in your true name, Lady Katherina De Vere. The money was always to be yours, despite the many people who attempted to re-write the past.

Your mother, Layla, was wed to my wretched son. He was a rogue among rogues, and I must take the blame for his insolence. Though no one can deny that you and your mother were punished in the severest, cruelest manner, something I wouldn't wish on my enemies. Pierce was—perhaps remains so to this day, only time will tell—a scoundrel, an abuser of women, and a deceiver. He broke his mother's heart, my precious Henrietta, and cast her into her dying role as a fiend. My dear girl, please know she was not always the heartless, cold, calculating woman Pierce turned her into. In the end, she could not bear to look upon your mother or you and think of the son who'd forsaken her, betrayed her, and felt no remorse. Henrietta thought to punish our son, but it did no good. He cared for nothing and no one except for perhaps himself.

I am not writing to make excuses for the cruelties forced upon you and your mother. No, I am here to make amends for it all in the only way an old, tired, lonely man can. I shall die alone, that is my cross to bear, and I am resigned to that fate.

For you, dear girl—despite my weakness in your infancy—I can at least provide a better fate.

Even back then, I attempted to do right by you. The vicar and his wife were good people, never blessed with a family of their own. I knew they would provide well for you and give you a home and a future away from Shrewbury, outside the reach of your father and my wife.

Kate folded the letter in her hands, unable to go on. She'd wanted to believe that it hadn't been as awful as her mother had explained. That perhaps A'laya had misunderstood something or misremembered everything.

Kate straightened her shoulders and unfolded the letter once more, finding where she'd left off.

I implore you, Katherina, do not be angry with your parents, the Elliotts. They took you in when Henrietta would have seen you thrown on the streets and forgotten. I could not allow that to happen, not to you, my precious granddaughter.

I was—am—a weak man.

I can only think that it is a common trait of the Shrewbury men.

It is far too late, as I well know. However, I must try to make amends before it is too late for me. After you were sent away to live with the vicar and his wife, nothing more than a tiny babe, I set up your trust with my solicitor with instructions that you were to be given this letter when you reached twenty-two, or in the event that you came looking. To you, I give everything within my power to give. The Shrewbury coffers in their entirety. Anything not entitled to the dukedom.

It is all yours, my dear Katherina.

Though I wish I had been strong and could have given you more.

My final request—if an old man of my debauched nature has any right to ask it—is that you please find your mother, Layla.

A'laya.

Kate turned the paper over in her hands, longing—searching—for more.

There was nothing else.

The letter was signed simply, *Walter*.

A tear slipped down her cheek, dripping onto the paper, causing the ink to smear and the final words to blend into a swirl of black.

Walter De Vere, the Duke of Shrewbury.

Her grandfather.

She and Joshua had learned enough about the people mentioned in her family's file to know that the old duke and his wife, Henrietta, were both long deceased. What Kate hadn't known was who had set up the trust that gave her the stipend and why. Now that she knew, she realized it didn't make the situation any clearer in her mind.

Kate and her mother had been pawns in a family feud that had started well before Kate had been born. Even before her mother had met and married Pierce De Vere if her mother's story about Pierce using his marriage to her as a way to thwart his mother were true.

Joshua sat on the lounge next to her. His familiar presence calmed her, not because she did not want to cry in front of him, but because she knew she could be weak with him. He would not judge her, nor would he turn away from her; he would not leave her to muddle through the mess others had made for Kate.

The urge to lean into Joshua and allow him to surround her with his warmth was nearly more than Kate could take.

"This was also in the parcel." He held another paper in his hand...a single sheet.

This one was clearly written by a meticulous hand, a steady quill, someone with some semblance of organization—unlike the letter from her grandfather.

Strange how easily she'd accepted the fact that she possessed a grandfather.

The page was a detailed list, signed at the bottom by a Mr. Caleb Abelston, Solicitor. He was the man listed in the file they'd found in Joshua's Bond Street office.

Kate scanned the document, her mind working to keep up with the extensive list, including a large sum of money, several properties, livestock, and antiquities.

"What is this, Joshua?" she asked, holding the paper out to him.

"It appears to be a list of assets. A bequeathal to you upon your twenty-second birthday." A note of awe tinged his tone as he scanned the page for a second time. "Henry and I will inquire into the matter first thing tomorrow morning."

"It is all mine," Kate mumbled. "He says it belongs to me."

That morning, Kate had fretted about her home, the schoolroom, and the means to repair it lest she find herself without a place to live.

In a few short hours, she'd discovered her true name, her ancestry, her mother, and the story of the devastating way they'd both been treated by the people that should have loved and cared for them. Kate hadn't had adequate time to allow the countess' presence to sink in, let alone discover that she was to inherit so much from a man she'd never even met.

Kate had gone from questioning who she was to learning truths about herself that only confused her more.

Joshua's stare was focused on her. Kate sensed it with a comforting warmth. Each time something happened, he offered help—never questioning her. Even now, she knew she could trust him.

When her fingers shook, Joshua took the envelope from her hand.

"May I?" he asked.

When she nodded, he unfolded the letter and read, his brow pulling low. "I am truly sorry, Kate."

"Sorry?" Kate's hand no longer quivered as she took the letter and the list back from Joshua. "There is no reason to be apologetic. We have the answers we've been searching for—or at least most of them. My mother found me, and it appears I am a wealthy woman."

All of her trouble *should* have evaporated. There *should* be a measure of finality with the information she'd gained. The weight of her responsibilities *should* be less.

Rationally, Kate comprehended how she should feel in that moment.

She should be happy. She should feel lighter and enlightened. She should bask in the new knowledge of her past. She should feel fulfilled in a way that had always escaped her.

Why then did she feel more alone and unbalanced than ever?

Why did she sense that she needed Joshua more than she ever had?

"I am happy you are here," she whispered. And she was. He was her constant, the one person she could count on to be who he was at all times. "I do not think I could wade through all of this alone."

"No one should be made to live their life alone." Joshua shifted on the lounge until he faced her, his legs brushing hers as he caressed her cheeks. His fingers were soft and warm against her chilled skin, reminding her of the press of his lips to her bare wrist. "We—you and I—were not made to be solitary creatures."

She longed for the sensation of his kiss once more, for Joshua to take her in his arms and banish all her concerns.

"I truly want to believe that is true." Kate covered his hand with hers, stopping him from pulling away from her. Her entire body screamed for her to hold tight, to not let him go—to demand they both realize there was far more between them than friendship. Kate wanted to belong to Joshua, which would, in turn, make him hers. They could face what came next together. They were stronger together than when they were apart. Kate felt that more and more each day.

His intense stare held hers as if he could read her thoughts and knew what she was thinking, and…

But that could not be.

Joshua was—had always been—a gentleman.

And Kate's thoughts were wanton and scandalous.

Leaning forward, Kate held her breath until her mouth met his. She hadn't any notion what she was doing or where it might lead, but she trusted Joshua enough to allow him to show her. Surprisingly, he didn't pull away from her. His hand moved from her cheek to the nape of her neck, his other wrapping around her back and pulling her closer.

When his lips parted, Kate melted. A sigh escaped her as she longed to be closer to him. But how could that be possible?

The rhythm of his lips dancing with hers promised there were many, many ways for Kate to be closer to him—both physically and emotionally.

Her hands grasped at his shoulders, her nails biting through the thin fabric of her gloves and into his coat. The undeniable draw between them only intensified when Kate adjusted until she sat on his lap, their lips never separating as she drew in the courage to slip her hands from his shoulders and into his hair.

A growl rumbled from his parted lips as if he very much liked the feel of her fingers in his strands.

Her mind—and her heart—thrummed with a new heat that seemed to coil tightly in the pit of her stomach.

All those parts of her that had been slowly crumbling from the moment Joshua rescued her from the fire began to meld back together, fusing so surely Kate suspected that no matter what came tomorrow, she'd never find herself weak to the point of falling apart again.

This man, this gloriously handsome and kind man in her arms, would make certain to hold her together through anything.

It was only when she'd literally questioned her entire existence that everything became clear to her.

The clock chimed on the mantel, and Joshua stiffened, his hands falling away from her as he drew back.

Kate stared up into his deep brown eyes. Shining back at her was a reflection of what she felt for him: love, adoration, longing, and, most of all…acceptance.

Without a single spoken word, Kate knew Joshua accepted her regardless of whether she was the daughter of a penniless vicar or a lord most foul. She wasn't certain who she was or who she wanted to be, and that was fine. It was more than fine because he would be with her while she figured it all out.

"Kate," Joshua whispered, shifting her on his lap as she rested her head against his shoulder.

"You are the bravest, kindest, most beautiful woman I've ever met. I understand you have much to learn, a lot to sort through, and it will take time. But—"

"*We* have much to learn," Kate said, the hint of a smile touching her lips. "And it can take all the time in the world as long as we do it together, you and I."

When he didn't immediately respond, Kate sat up straighter, her head leaving his shoulder. Not for a second did she fear he would shy away from her assertion.

And she was correct.

In answer to her proclamation, Joshua pulled her close again, his kiss an unspoken agreement. A promise that needed no words.

CHAPTER 16

JOSHUA WAVED TO Kate and her mother as they paused outside the schoolroom to look back at him before entering the building. It continued to take him by surprise each time the women stood close to each other. The resemblance was unmistakable even with the years separating the pair. The last thing Joshua wanted was to spend even a minute without Kate by his side; however, there was work to be done, and he would join the two women as quickly as his day allowed.

The newly acquainted pair also needed time together. They'd lost nearly twenty years, and it would be no small feat to overcome the time and distance between them to forge a genuine familial bond. The immense level of joy he felt for Kate and all she'd discovered brimmed inside him. She was happy, too. Joshua knew it. However, there was still much confusion for her to work through.

The why of it all had been answered, but so many questions remained.

And it would likely take time to uncover it all.

Thankfully, with the letter from Walter, the Duke of Shrewbury, written before his passing, Kate had all the time and funds needed to set her own pace with the discovery. Joshua was content and more than willing to let Kate guide them through the new revelations.

Joshua smiled, taking in the bustling street around him where men and women hurried down the walkways, rode horses down the lane, and went about their days.

Looking forward once more, he noted that Kate and the countess had disappeared into the schoolroom.

The quicker Joshua handled the matter of the old duke's letter, the swifter he could rejoin Kate.

He'd never been one to succumb to such all-encompassing feelings for a woman. But Kate made Joshua want to throw caution to the wind and embrace wherever their attraction might take them. She'd fit perfectly in his arms the previous night, and he hadn't wanted to let her go. But he knew that if Dolly or another servant happened upon them in such a situation, the gossip would spread quickly, and Joshua did not want that for Kate.

Joshua turned and entered his office, greeting Henry with a bit more enthusiasm than was typical. "Good morning, Henry. I do hope your evening was satisfactory."

His assistant stood, gave Joshua a curt bow, and then glanced over his shoulder to Joshua's office.

Light shone from the partially open door.

"My lord," Henry's voice was a tentative

whisper. "You have a visitor in your office."

"A visitor?" Joshua stared past Henry, ignoring the young man's unease. Unfortunately, whoever awaited him was out of sight. "My first client isn't expected for another hour, and I have some work to do…"

Henry cleared his throat, his voice dropping lower than before. "He insisted it is a matter of great import."

"The man's name?" Joshua mentally counted the number of people and businesses he'd contacted of late. Most were linked to Kate—the bank, the Shrewbury estate, and the matter of Walter's letter.

Grabbing a card from his desk, Henry handed it to Joshua. The paper was thick with an embossed name printed in gold leaf on the fine card.

Mr. Daniel Burns, Solicitor.

Joshua had heard of the man. He had been at Oxford a few years before Joshua. His family held one of the most prestigious law offices in London and were rumored to handle matters for the Bank of England, Barclays, and *The London Gazette*. The family had wealth and means with many connections even Joshua's father could not boast about.

Why would the man be in Cheapside awaiting an audience with Joshua?

"Lord Joshua Stuart?" Burns sauntered into the main office and halted several feet from Joshua, a folder under his arm.

Never had Joshua felt like an interloper in his own building; however, the way Burns looked perfectly at ease despite having no appointment made Joshua apprehensive.

"How can I be of assistance, Mr. Burns?" Joshua, attempting to take back control of the situation, walked forward and gestured toward his office. "We can speak privately in my office."

Joshua took in the room once they'd both entered, and he'd closed the door behind them. Everything appeared as it had the night before. His desk was orderly, and chairs lined the room, ready for class to be held later in the morning after Kate had finished across the street.

Neither man sat, each preferring to stand.

"My lord, am I correct that your client is Miss Katherina Elliott?" Burns clasped his hands behind his back, the file still under his arm as his serious stare assessed Joshua. When Joshua nodded, the man continued. "I received word from the Bank of England concerning your client's request for funds pertaining to the Shrewbury estate."

"That is correct." Joshua eyed the solicitor. His finely tailored suit appeared freshly pressed, and his cravat was expertly arranged. "Are you a solicitor for the bank?"

Burns barked with a sharp chuckle. "Heavens, no."

Joshua's brow rose in question.

The solicitor retrieved the file from under his arm, opening it to reveal several pages of handwritten notes. "I am here on behalf of the Earl of Holderness, Pierce De Vere. He is the heir to the Shrewbury dukedom, previously run by his late father. He has recently returned to London, and we are preparing to petition the Lord Chancellor for a writ of summons to the House of Lords. Unfortunately, there is a small matter that must be rectified before that can happen."

"Holderness is in London?" Joshua suppressed his shock, knowing Burns would use it to his client's advantage if he were thrown off guard. "I heard it has been many years since the man has been seen or heard. At least, in England."

Burns snapped the folder closed and slipped it back under his arm. "Yes, well, circumstances have arisen, and my client believes it is in his best interest to reclaim his place among society and take over his father's estate."

"What circumstances exactly, if you do not mind me inquiring?" Had the man created another scandal and been forced to return to London? Or had he squandered away whatever funds he had?

"It is a delicate, personal matter."

"If you are here, I can only assume you know of the late duke's wishes made before his passing."

Burns shrugged. "The earl only seeks what is rightfully his and then wishes to be on his way without further inconveniencing Miss Katherina."

"Do you not mean, Lady Katherina De Vere—his daughter?" Joshua was done tiptoeing around the solicitor's true motives for the visit.

"I am uncertain where you have gained your information, Stuart. However, I have no documentation proving that the earl has ever been wed, let alone fathered a child."

It was Joshua's turn to chuckle. The dry laugh was nearly a growl. "You have seen the letter then."

"A letter written by a man who was certainly not of sound, stable mind." Burns' eyes narrowed. "It is highly unlikely that anyone would see the letter as anything more than the senseless ramblings of a man losing his mind with grief over the loss of his wife and his son's departure from England. There is no proof my client was ever wed, and even if Miss Katherina were deemed an illegitimate offspring, she would not legally be entitled to anything from the dukedom. However, I have a proposition for Miss Katherina…"

He could only imagine the *proposition* a fiend like Holderness would offer Kate. The man had wed and then abandoned his young bride when she was with child, leaving her in the hands of the duchess, arguably a worse foe. The vision of Joshua physically throwing Burns from his office flashed through Joshua's mind, yet something stopped him.

Holderness was in London.

As was Katherina.

As was her mother, A'laya.

Did the earl know of his wife's presence in town? Was it a combination of Joshua inquiring with the bank and A'laya's reappearance that had instigated Burns' arrival at Joshua's Cheapside office?

A wolfish grin crossed Burns' face. He obviously took Joshua's silence as confirmation that he was prepared to entertain whatever ludicrous proposition the scheming pair had devised to once again cheat Kate and her mother out of what rightfully belonged to them.

The solicitor made a show of unbuttoning his jacket and retrieving an envelope from the inside pocket, though he did not hand it to Joshua. "I have prepared a document for Miss Katherina El—"

"Lady Katherina De Vere," Joshua corrected, his chin raising a notch in challenge.

"Call the woman what you wish, as long as she signs the paper." Burns waved off the correction before continuing. "If your client signs the document, my client is prepared to pay her handsomely for it."

Certainly not as handsomely as what the deceased duke bequeathed her, Joshua thought. "How much?"

"Twenty thousand pounds, given at one time," Burns said, his arrogance bordering on absurd.

Perhaps the solicitor and Holderness were not privy to Walter's letter, after all. The sum was laughable compared to what Katherina had been promised.

If either gentleman thought that Joshua would agree to such a paltry sum for everything the women had endured, they were the ones not of sound mind.

"Have we an agreement?" Burns prodded, his agitation brimming.

"What is it you wish signed?" It was Joshua's turn to push back. The solicitor obviously needed the document endorsed. When he did not answer Joshua's question, he leaned his hip against his desk, anger flaring in the solicitor's eyes. "I cannot bring something to my client without some explanation of what it is she is to sign and the benefits it offers to her—if it truly *does* benefit her."

"I can take the matter before the courts. The settlement is generous, considering the girl wasn't aware before a few days ago that she was the granddaughter of a duke," Burns scoffed. "She was raised in Cheapside, for heaven's sake. And now she thinks she *deserves* my client's inheritance? Every court in the land will see her for what she is."

"Which is?" Joshua's hands balled into fists, and he slipped them behind his back to hide his anger at Burns' words. The solicitor was the type of man who took pleasure in upsetting others.

"Please share, Mr. Burns."

"A status-seeking hoyden who does not deserve the title of *lady*." The matter-of-fact tone in the solicitor's declaration enraged Joshua until his vision blurred.

"My client only just learned her true identity." Joshua spoke slowly, deliberately, begging his anger to subside, and his mind to clear. "Between you and I"—Joshua paused, working to release his built-up tension—"the sum is large for a woman of Katherina's current means. There must be more to the situation. I am the son of a duke, Burns, I understand how things go, more than most."

Joshua sensed the animosity Burns directed at him swiftly turn to comradery.

He'd convinced the solicitor that, as a peer, Joshua knew the overreaching hand of those beneath him. It was exactly as he wanted Holderness' man to think.

Burns seemed resigned. He stuffed the envelope back into his breast pocket and re-opened the folder he held, taking out a single sheet of paper and handing it to Joshua.

The handwriting was similar to the letter Kate had received the night before, but the script was nowhere near as erratic. This had been written with great thought, not the impending urgency of a man who saw his end in sight.

It was the Duke of Shrewbury's officially recorded last will and testament.

Much of the single page read as many of the wills Joshua drafted in his time with Stuart and Lords did. A list of assets, properties, investments, sums of money owed to others, as well as a few notes owed to the dukedom. There was mention of livestock, crops, and tenants—yearly repair and maintenance figures for a farming property near the town of Bampton, Oxfordshire. The Shrewbury dukedom was not the wealthiest title he'd seen, but it was far from being considered impoverished.

Toward the bottom of the page, Shrewbury's script turned bold as if he'd pressed the quill into the paper a bit too hard. The section was only a few sentences, and Joshua scanned the words before his stare darted to the beginning once more to read with purpose.

I, the Duke of Shrewbury, of sound mind and body, do so intend and decree that all my worldly possessions, property, and funds not entitled to the dukedom are herein bequeathed to Lady Katherina De Vere, also known herein as Miss Katherina Elliott of Cheapside, the only child of the Earl of Holderness, Pierce De Vere. As of this decree, my heir apparent's absence from polite society is known to all of England. If in the event that my son, Pierce, returns to England, he may inherit one-half of all non-entitled possessions, property, and funds if two stipulations are met:

The Earl of Holderness agrees to find and make amends with his only daughter, Lady Katherina De Vere

The Earl of Holderness returns to his responsibilities without tarnished name or reputation.

If the heir apparent to the Shrewbury dukedom does not wholly agree and execute these wishes, he shall not inherit anything but the title of duke and Shrewbury Gardens itself. He will forfeit all else to Lady Katherina De Vere.

In the unfortunate event that Lady Katherina De Vere expires before the heir to the Shrewbury dukedom, Pierce De Vere shall be granted the Shrewbury estate in its entirety.

Joshua read the final sentence several times.

If Kate perished, Holderness inherited everything: possessions, wealth, and property—without question.

"Has the earl seen this document?" Joshua asked.

Burns plucked the will from Joshua's hands and tucked it back into the folder before closing it. "Of course, he received it a few weeks ago."

"Mr. Daniel Burns," Joshua roared. "Where in the bloody hell is your *client*?"

CHAPTER 17

A'LAYA STOOD IN the small room off the main area of the schoolroom where tables and chairs had once filled the space. There was still a prevalent, acidic aroma in the air; however, with time, it would grow less and less pronounced until it was gone entirely. The damaged floorboards had been removed, as well as the scorched walls. Her daughter had shared on their carriage ride to Cheapside that a new door and front window would soon replace the gaping holes in the part of the building that faced the street.

It was nearly inconceivable that Kate—A'laya was slowly adjusting to her daughter's preferred name—had been asleep upstairs during it all.

The metal at her neck heated as it often did when A'laya thought of her daughter.

Before yesterday, it had been nothing more

than a deep-seated longing that she feared would never be realized. Yet, now, only a dozen feet away, Kate moved a wood rocking chair toward the stairs. The intricately carved back had been charred in the blaze. The chair must have meant a great deal to Kate because she lifted it with a loving touch, not allowing the curved bottom to scrape the newly nailed-down floorboards.

There was so much A'laya had yet to learn about Kate. Her questions seemed endless.

Though, despite that, she remained quiet, happy to simply watch the daughter she'd never thought to see again. There would be time— years ahead of them—to discuss everything they'd missed in each other's lives. Their future was endless. For now, A'laya was content to just be in Kate's presence.

And what a presence her daughter possessed.

It was as if she didn't realize the command she held over every room she entered. It was subtle but evident. Servants in Lord Stuart's home had found every occasion to speak with Kate. When they arrived in Cheapside, a pair of ladies greeted Kate with an embrace. It hadn't surprised A'laya in the slightest that Lord Stuart kept watch on Kate until they'd safely entered the schoolroom. Only then had he turned to his own building.

A'laya had spent a great many years plagued with nightmares. In some, Kate lived in squalor, hungry, filthy, and without love. In others, her daughter had been deposited in a home for abandoned children. Once, she'd dreamt of finding a tiny cross on Shrewbury land and was forced to accept her daughter had been lost to her forever.

It gave her some semblance of peace to know

that Kate had been raised in a loving home with a mother and father who adored her, cared for her, and made sure she had an education and a home. They'd loved Kate as their own. This had given A'laya pause, but any lingering strings of jealousy over the vicar and his wife being given the gift of loving Kate had diminished as quickly as they appeared. It hadn't been their fault that Kate had been stolen from A'laya. That was the Duke and Duchess of Shrewbury's doing. They were the villainous pair, not the Elliotts.

A'laya allowed herself to envy the couple's years raising her daughter, but jealousy was not warranted.

They'd protected Kate in a way no one had safeguarded A'laya after she met Pierce and left her family home.

She stooped to pick up an assortment of books that were scattered haphazardly across the small room.

She recalled the story Kate had relayed to her, and a shudder went down her spine at the thought of Kate and Joshua being trapped with no way out.

"I can collect those." Kate rushed over and took the books A'laya had managed to pick up. "I did not invite you to accompany me for the day only to put you to work. Please, sit down. The upstairs has been deemed usable. You can lie down if needed, or I can set water to boil for tea."

The empathy in Kate's sparkling grey-blue eyes pained A'laya more than her aching back.

"I am not one to lounge about when things need to be done."

Kate smiled, and for a brief moment, A'laya's heart stopped beating, and she was transported to another time and place.

"What?" Kate dipped and collected a few

more books.

"You have your grandmother's smile," A'laya confessed. She was thrilled to not see a speck of Pierce in the woman. "You have her eyes, too."

Kate met her stare, scrutinizing A'laya's own countenance. "I have *your* eyes."

"I did not seek to be so bold," A'laya said with a laugh.

If anyone had told A'laya a fortnight prior she'd be standing in a room, chatting and laughing with her daughter, A'laya would have thought the person deranged.

"Tell me of your family," Kate asked lightly, busying herself around the room.

A'laya had wanted to pour her heart out since finding Kate the day before. She'd wanted to shout it from on high and share everything about her past and that of their home country. She'd longed to ask Kate if she'd been treated differently than the other children because of her differences, if she'd wondered all these years where she'd inherited her creamy, tan skin, curling, black hair, and captivating, grey-blue eyes. What of the freckles that no doubt sprinkled across the bridge of her nose and cheeks when she spent too much time in the sun? Did she loathe them or love them?

Yet, deeper than her outward appearance, A'laya saw the internal similarities between she and her daughter.

Even without A'laya, Kate had become a self-assured, independent, generous, and intelligent woman. This was evident in how she'd taken care of herself in the years since her parents' passing.

A'laya would have been lost and desolate if she'd been left with neither of her parents. She'd been naïve and susceptible to Pierce's lies, going so far as to ignore her mother's warning of the man. However, A'laya had thought herself in love, and she possessed the same determined streak she recognized in her daughter.

"I am unsure where to begin." A'laya sat in one of the few chairs that hadn't burnt entirely in the fire. She rubbed at her chest; the ache that should have disappeared with the discovery of Katherina still causing pain. "There is so much to say."

"Why not tell me about your necklace?" Kate nodded to where A'laya unknowingly rubbed at the metal. "I have seen a picture of it before."

"You have?" A'laya glanced down at the simple adornment that'd hung around her neck since childhood. "It was a gift from my mother. She bought it for me while we walked the merchants' stalls when I was a child."

"What does it mean?"

"It is the Path of Life." A'laya felt Kate's stare as it followed the intricate swirls and circles, likely thinking the same as A'laya had when she first saw the symbol. "My mother once said, 'The paths are the circles. See the center rings? They go on forever. That is who you are. No matter what happens, you are always A'laya. Your mama's daughter, your grandmother's grandchild, and your father's precious baby girl. You will make choices, little one. But know you are always loved for who you are.'"

A'laya closed her eyes, a sadness burrowing deep into her chest at the words that had kept her focused for so many years, even during the long nights and even longer winters without Katherina.

"The necklace was drawn on the back of a piece of paper in the file we found at Joshua's office," Kate said. "It seemed very important at the time, as if I knew the symbol but could not place it."

"I am sorry I was not there for you." A'laya hung her head. "While we were not together, you were still my Katherina. I thought of you every moment, dreamt of you every night, and prayed relentlessly to find you."

"Mayhap I did the same without realizing it," Kate whispered.

"I grew up with stories of the fierce, strong women of our past. Yet, I was weak. I allowed a fiend to deceive me, to trick me so completely I believed he loved me." She paused, lifting her chin until she stared up at Kate. "But you, my blessed daughter, are everything I was unable to be. For that, I am eternally grateful."

"I do not feel fierce or strong."

A'laya sensed that it was her fault despite her absence. That she was the reason Kate did not fully comprehend her strength. "How can you say that?"

Kate held her arms wide, gesturing to the schoolroom. "I nearly lost everything, and it is only because of Joshua's kindness—and the funds from Shrewbury—that I can make the necessary repairs. If it were not for Joshua, I do not know where I would be. I did not question anything. I did not know where to turn when it all happened. Heavens, I did not even know that my home was burning until Joshua came for me."

Each time her daughter spoke of the solicitor, the light within her brightened. "Lord Joshua Stuart is a good man."

A'laya fell silent, allowing Kate to think on all she'd said. Upon meeting the man, she'd thought him her foe. She'd been taken aback to find that she trusted him almost immediately, even before she took his palm and made to read the lord. There was much a person could gain from merely requesting to hold another's hand. Those who balked at the contact were most often to be avoided. Those who did not readily offer up their hand were generally hiding something. It was rare—very rare indeed—that a man held out his hand as Lord Stuart had, without question, hesitation, or reservations.

Kate glanced toward the front of the schoolroom.

A'laya's chest contracted at the forlorn look in her daughter's eyes. She'd seen it in her own over the long, hard years. It was the look of a woman who wanted something very badly but was resigned to never have it.

In A'laya's case, it had been *someone*. Her daughter.

In Kate's case, A'laya suspected it was also about someone.

Joshua.

"You should go to him," A'laya whispered, staring toward the front of the room and out the open doorway.

Kate feigned confusion. "Go to whom?"

A'laya saw directly through the ploy. "The solicitor."

They'd been reacquainted only a short time; however, she truly felt as if she knew the young woman before her. Her hopes, her dreams, her fears. Because they matched many of A'laya's from the past.

On cue, Kate's cheeks blossomed with heat at A'laya's direct answer. "No, I cannot. He had work to do, and I've inconvenienced him enough."

There was no fooling A'laya. In fact, the

solicitor hadn't even attempted to hide his attraction for Kate. Attraction... She scoffed. What Joshua felt for Kate was far more than simple lust—and just as complicated. Maybe more so. The interest and captivation were duly returned by her daughter. One did not have to claim any type of extra senses or gifts to see the connection between the two.

A budding love that would soon bring Kate to her senses. Very unlike the speedy courtship and duplicity of A'laya's relationship with Pierce.

There was only authenticity behind the stolen looks exchanged between Kate and Joshua.

"You are not an inconvenience to him, my girl."

Kate shook her head. "He, as well as his uncle, was friends with my parents. He feels responsible for me. Needs to make certain I do well."

"It is more than that." A'laya shook her head. "Your hand, my daughter."

Kate's eyes widened, but she came forth and offered her bare hand to A'laya. Both had stripped their gloves when they began working, and the feel of her daughter's soft skin against her rough, calloused, wrinkled flesh was welcome. Very welcome, indeed.

Straightening her shoulders, A'laya stared into Kate's eerily familiar eyes and took in her creamy complexion—just the right strength of tea with milk. She did not want to let her go. She smiled, squeezed her daughter's hand, and brought it closer as she traced the lines in Katherina's palm.

"Ahhh," she cooed. "Methinks you know more than you speak, Kate. Tell me, have you and the solicitor spoken of your connection?"

"Not in so many words." The blush returned, only hints detectable high on her cheekbones as she averted her stare. "But, yes. And I think if things were"—she paused, lifting her chin—"different, mayhap we…"

"What, my dear girl?"

"Before…before I knew who I was or anything about you, I thought our stations in life were what would keep us apart." A rigid kind of acceptance overtook Kate, and A'laya noted the way her daughter's eyes cleared. "But now…now I know it is so much more. Not only do I not know who I am, but I do not know where I belong. How can I bring Joshua into that? It is not fair. Not to him and certainly not to you. We have only just met, and it is you who needs me."

A'laya laughed, the chuckle rumbling deeply within her until her shoulders ached. She released her grip on Kate's hand. "We have much time—years—to spend together. I will never leave you again unless you request it of me—"

Stark fear darkened Kate's face. "I would never."

A'laya lifted her hand to pat Kate's cheek, something her mother had done to her when she became anxious in her youth. She let her hand fall to her side, uncertain if it was the right thing to do. "What I am attempting to say is that I will not leave you. But Lord Stuart, he is a kind and generous man. One with a heart larger than I've encountered in anyone since my father's passing. You should not let anything stand in your way if he is the man you desire. And if it is love that draws your heart to him, do not wait another moment to tell him."

If anyone knew how quickly life could change, and so drastically you might not even recognize yourself or your surroundings, it was A'laya. In the blink of an eye, she'd gone from an innocent young woman to a scorned wife, abandoned with a babe in an unfamiliar home. Before she'd been able to reconcile her new reality, that had been stolen from her, as well.

Fate was not always kind.

Fortune could not be counted on to be in Kate's favor.

Neither fate nor fortune had treated A'laya well in the past. But Kate was not A'laya, despite both women having found men they loved. A'laya's husband had been a selfish man, yet all she'd witnessed of the solicitor were acts of kindness and altruism. Pierce was a scoundrel who'd mistreated and betrayed A'laya. Lord Stuart was not the earl, and A'laya needed to make Kate understand that fact.

THE OPEN AND honest encouragement from her mother—Kate still could scarcely believe she could call the older woman that—had Kate rethinking everything that pertained to Joshua. Undoubtedly, she felt a certain, *unexplainable* draw toward him; however, it could not be as simple as all of that.

Yes, she desired him. Greatly.

Yes, he had been her constant for longer than she realized.

Yes, their kiss had stirred feelings and emotions in Kate that far exceeded lust.

She'd noted him watching her on their ride into Cheapside. Though she hadn't dared glance over her shoulder, she'd felt his eyes on her as she and A'laya had journeyed across the street to the schoolroom. Even in this moment, she suspected that if she glanced out the open doorway, she'd glimpse him in the window across the street.

Surprisingly, Kate felt comforted by his presence and attention. For the first time in recent years, everything was not her burden to carry alone. Never, not once, had Joshua given her the impression that she and her life's circumstances were a hardship for him.

When had Kate begun to crave Joshua's presence?

"Do you love him?" A'laya whispered.

Love? Kate had loved her parents, the vicar and his wife. She knew she was already coming to love the woman standing before her. But to love a man? Kate had never seen such a thing in her future. It was a dream she hadn't allowed herself to believe could be hers.

Yet, the truth was undeniable.

No matter the uncertainty in her life, Kate was convinced of one thing: she *was* in love with Joshua.

Her mother smiled. "Oh, my girl. I do believe he loves you, too."

"How can you be certain?" Kate wasn't convinced her feelings for Joshua were reciprocated. Yet, A'laya, who'd only just met him the previous day, seemed confident.

"He looks at you the way my father did with my mother. He cares for you, thinks only of you, even when the easier decision would be to remain detached." A'laya sighed, a forlorn sadness creeping into her expression. "He is everything I longed for in my youth."

"Did my father...?" Kate swallowed,

knowing that despite Walter's letter, she needed to hear it from her mother. "He must have loved you at some point."

"I thought he did." A'laya's smile was heartbreaking. "He was everything I'd dreamt of in a husband: handsome, dashing, charming, titled, and he lavished me with gifts. At least he did in those very early days of our courtship. It was all a ruse, a way to ensnare me, and, worst of all, punish his mother for withholding his allowance."

"Did the duke tell you this?" Kate had been gaining the courage to share with A'laya the letter Walter had left for her. Not because she did not trust the older woman with the knowledge, but because reliving the pain of those early years might very well be too much for A'laya to bear. She never should have had to endure it in the first place. How could Kate allow her to read the damning evidence of it all written in black ink by the duke's own hand? "I mean—"

A'laya held up her hand, and Kate fell silent. "He did not have to speak any of it. The duchess was keen on making sure I knew that Pierce's heart and loyalty had never been with me. Even after he disappeared to London before your birth, it was evident our marriage had never been the serendipitous event I'd believed it to be. I was an utter fool, little more than a senseless girl who could not see Pierce for the nefarious lord he was. But you, Katherina, you are not that girl. You are a woman, a lady who knows her worth and that of others. Your heart knows that what you feel for Lord Stuart is true, even if your mind has yet to accept it."

"I wish we hadn't been separated all those years ago." A tear spilled unbidden down Kate's cheek, and A'laya brushed it away.

"I think, mayhap, fate had plans for you even before you were born, my dear girl." A'laya rubbed at her necklace before reaching around her neck and untying the twine that secured the treasured keepsake. "If you'd remained with me, you might not have crossed paths with your solicitor, and we might have suffered more at the duchess's hands. We would have had one another, but you may not have found love."

Kate's chest swelled, filling in a way she'd never known it could. She'd grown up with a certain detachment from everything and everyone around her, even her parents to an extent. Finally, she was coming to understand who she was, where she'd come from, and most importantly, where she belonged.

It wasn't a place, though she loved her tiny schoolroom.

It wasn't Cheapside, though she had an affinity for her pupils and those she'd come to meet and know in the area.

Where she belonged had everything to do with who was by her side.

No matter if they resided in England—or the New World—Kate belonged at Joshua's side. And he at hers. She suddenly knew it with certainty.

The silent exchange they'd shared the previous night made more sense as Kate accepted the startling reality.

"Mother, I think I should go—"

"Go to him, Katherina," A'laya said with a grin.

Kate embraced her mother, lingering in the soft, welcoming embrace before stepping back.

She needed to speak with Joshua and tell him how she felt. Their silent pledge was no longer all she wanted. It was only when she spoke to him of her love that she'd know the extent of his feelings for her.

"I will return," Kate called over her shoulder with a wave as she started for the door.

She hurried across the room, making certain to watch her step on the loose floorboards. As she neared the front of the building, a shadow crossed the threshold, and a man stepped into her boarded-up school, the light from outside momentarily shrouding his face from view.

He was a familiar stranger, that much Kate knew. It wasn't Joshua, Henry, or one of his other servants, but the man's height and set of his broad shoulders were vaguely familiar.

The hairs on the back of her neck stood on end when A'laya gasped behind her.

Kate missed the name her mother called into the nearly empty schoolroom, but as she turned back toward her mother, the man swung his arm, his fist connecting with Kate's left temple.

Lights exploded before her eyes as she careened backwards, her arms flailing for something to steady herself but finding nothing in the bare room. Her head swam and burst with pain when it knocked against the floorboards.

Her arm was wrenched upward as she was pulled to her feet, but she could not bring herself to open her eyes as the bursts of colored light faded until all she saw was pitch-black.

As she allowed herself to embrace the darkness and ward off the pain, Kate heard her mother scream…

"Pierce!"

CHAPTER 18

KATE CAME TO slowly, her vision blurred to the point where she needed to close her eyes to concentrate with her other senses. She smelled the remnants of a fire. She was still in the schoolroom, but perhaps upstairs? The room was frigid, as made evident by her numb fingers. The sounds of labored breathing permeated the room. The only other sounds to be heard were the passing carriages and horses on the street below, but even that was muffled. She must be in the room farthest from the road and near the mews.

Wiggling her foot, Kate realized that she was sitting in a chair; the toe of her shoe grazed the wooden floor. They must be in the small kitchen area. She leaned forward slightly, only to find something sharp and unpleasant press into her neck just below her chin.

"Do not move, Katherina," A'laya whispered

hoarsely.

The scrape of a chair across the floorboards sounded not far from Kate.

"Yes, *Katherina*, listen to your *mother*," a male voice hissed in her ear.

"Let her go, you fiend!"

"Do shut up, you caterwauling shrew." Whatever the man held at her throat receded until Kate barely felt the pain of its sharp point. "Now, Katherina, why could you not simply have perished in the fire? It would have saved me a lot of trouble, and you much pain."

She slowly opened her eyes. As she focused, she peered into A'laya's hardened stare. Her mother's rigid posture and penetrating gaze did not hide the tears that seeped from her eyes as she glared at the man behind Kate. Her mother, likely much the same as Kate, sat in one of the chairs that were usually tucked close to the tiny table that Kate and her parents had dined at in her youth.

She moved her arms a bit and twisted slightly. Nothing bound her to the chair but the threat of the blade at her throat. It was the same thing that kept her mother frozen in the chair across from her.

"However, I do see the advantage of having both of you here at the same time," the man drawled, drawing out each word with agonizing slowness. "Doing away with just one meddlesome female would not have solved my problems, I understand that now."

Terror must have shone in Kate's eyes because her mother mouthed the word, "*Sorry*," over and over again.

"It isn't your fault," Kate declared, the blade cutting into her neck once more. A fiery trail snaked down her throat and under the collar of her blouse. There was little doubt who the man at her back was. Pierce De Vere—her father. And he'd set the fire that had nearly killed her.

Now, he'd returned for a second attempt at doing away with her.

Only now did Kate understand why he'd seek to do it. She was nearly old enough to have received Walter's letter when her bequest ran out, and her full inheritance was made available to her.

And her mother was in trouble, too.

"Please, let A'laya go," Kate pleaded. She knew it would do no good, and if anything of the man were to be believed, he was not above being cruel for cruelty's sake, but she had to try. "She stands to inherit nothing from the Shrewbury estate, and I don't even know her."

"Do you think me simpleminded?" the earl snarled.

"You certainly are not an intelligent man," Kate prodded, only achieving a quick press of the blade before he once again eased back. "What do you want?"

"What do I want?" His tone was deranged, his pitch rising with each word. "I want what is rightfully mine. What I earned."

"Earned?" A'laya scoffed. "You've earned nothing, you treacherous beast."

Pierce stood behind Kate, the knife leaving her throat as he rushed at A'laya, the blade pointed at her.

"Don't touch her," Kate screamed, kicking out her leg until it tangled with his, sending him off balance as quickly as his punch had knocked her down earlier. "Run!"

As he slammed into the table, bashing his hip against the unforgiving wooden top, he cursed.

Kate glanced at her mother but noticed that she hadn't run. Instead, she stood, grasping the chair with both of her hands as she swung it, catching the fiend in the knees. He collapsed.

There was no time to commend A'laya on her accurate blow.

Pierce's howl of pain echoed in the small room as he fought to gain purchase on the table while still keeping the knife in his grasp.

Kate attempted to make her way past Pierce and toward A'laya to the door of the upstairs' landing behind her. Pierce halted her, swinging out his arm and swiping the knife at her thigh, ripping through her skirt. Kate grabbed at the area, staggering back, but the blade hadn't made it through her underpinnings to cut her flesh.

"You bastard!" Her mother darted past Pierce and took hold of the copper pot from the pellet stove. "I will never allow you to harm Katherina again."

A'laya held the cookware high above her head and brought it down, crushing Pierce in the shoulder.

He dropped, and the knife skittered across the floor into the far corner.

When he didn't immediately move, Kate lifted her stare to her mother's enraged face as she seethed with anger, her heavy breathing audible even over the pounding of footfalls on the stairs.

"Mother," Kate said, rushing to catch A'laya before her knees gave out from her trembling and she tumbled to the floor. "Are you hurt?"

"No, child." A'laya rubbed at her shoulder as Kate slipped her arm around her mother's waist to help support her.

"What in the bloody hell?" Joshua rushed into the room, out of breath from his dash up the stairs, another man close on his heels. His face drained of color when he spotted Pierce crumpled on the floor. "Kate, A'laya, are you both okay?"

"Go to him, Katherina," A'laya whispered. When Kate trained her gaze on her mother, A'laya continued, "Go, I will be fine. Sore from my old age, but I am well. Very well, indeed."

With a smile, Kate kissed her mother lightly on the cheek, surprising even herself with the intimate gesture.

Kate skirted the room, staying out of Pierce's reach even though he groaned in a heap on the floor and, with Joshua's arrival, proved no further threat to anyone, especially Kate.

"Joshua." Kate threw herself at him, and he opened his arms wide to catch her. She didn't fear for even a moment that he wouldn't bundle her close and press a kiss to her forehead, her cheek, and finally her lips. After a few moments, she pulled back and cupped his face between her hands. "Joshua Stuart, I am utterly, completely, and madly in love with you! I don't want another minute to pass without you knowing that my whole heart belongs to you."

"And he'd best take great care with it," her mother called from behind Kate. They both turned to catch her mother's wink. "I wouldn't relish bashing him over the head with a pot, but I will not hesitate if the need arises. So, what do you say, my lord?"

"I love her with complete abandon."

"Do not tell me. Tell my daughter, you charming lord!" Her mother chuckled.

"Burns!" Pierce pushed to sit, his back against the leg of the table as he craned his neck to stare up at the well-dressed gentleman who'd followed Joshua up the stairs. "Burns! Send for the magistrate at once. This wench"—he pointed a shaking finger in A'laya's direction—"whacked me over the head with that copper pot."

"Fortune was on your side, you scoundrel. I only caught you in the shoulder." A'laya stepped toward her treacherous husband, and Kate feared she might finish the job she'd started. "If you give Katherina any more trouble, I will not miss my mark again."

"I said, send for the magistrate, Burns," Pierce seethed. "I have been attacked and will not stand for it. I am to be given my father's title soon enough, and assaulting a peer is not acceptable."

Now out of danger, Kate took a closer look at the man who was her father. She didn't see even an ounce of herself in him, yet she recognized the man from when she and the school children had walked to the bookseller before the fire. He had been outside the cobbler's shop.

He had set the fire. It had nothing to do with the cobbler and their argument.

"My lord." Burns scurried over to assist Pierce to his feet. Once he'd dusted the man off, he turned back to Joshua, but his penetrating stare landed on Kate. Immediately, the man's stare softened. "Lady Katherina De Vere?" He gave her a curt bow, not waiting for her acknowledgement. "Your neck, it is bloodied."

"That blackguard hit her and held a knife to her throat." A'laya took a menacing step toward Pierce. It did not matter that the man was twice her size with wide, barrel-like arms.

"I am sending for the magistrate this instant." The man spun on his heel and started for the door before pausing. "Stuart, you will do me a great service if you would hold the earl

here until I return with the magistrate. We will
need to take written statements from Lady
Katherina and..." He glanced over at Kate's
mother in question.

"The Countess of Holderness," Joshua filled
in. "Lady Holderness, Lady Katherina, allow me
to introduce Mr. Daniel Burns, Solicitor."

"My lady," Burns nodded in respect. "We
need to gather their statements for the magistrate
before he takes the earl before the Lord High
Steward."

"Take—take—take me where?" Pierce
stuttered.

"I will see you held responsible for these
crimes, my lord." The steely edge to Burns' voice
had Kate instantly liking the solicitor. Without
another word, Burns departed the room, and his
footsteps could be heard hurrying down the
stairs.

"This is a travesty. The likes of you do not
have any right to hold me."

When he attempted to follow Burns, her
mother took hold of the copper pot and shook it
at him while Joshua grabbed the earl's arms and
wrenched them behind his back.

"I suggest you remain silent and do not
attempt to flee," Joshua warned. "I can say I am
not above allowing the countess to have another
shot at you."

Kate crossed her arms, blocking the doorway
as they waited for Burns to return.

It took only a few minutes before Joshua's
driver and assistant rushed up the stairs and
took over the watch of her father, freeing Kate,
Joshua, and her mother to return to the office
across the street.

Until that point, Kate hadn't allowed the
danger of their situation to sink in. However, by

the time Joshua closed the door behind them, and they all sat to await the magistrate, her entire body trembled with shock, and her hand felt for the shallow slice at her throat.

She was fortunate…they were all lucky.

Joshua pulled her into his side, wrapping his arms about her waist as she leaned her head on his shoulder. In truth, she'd never doubted that Joshua would come for them, even if her mother hadn't managed to get hold of the copper pot.

Between Joshua and her mother, Kate had the family, the love, and the connection she'd felt lacking all these years.

She loved her mother in the natural way any daughter would, despite their many years apart.

And Joshua, she loved him with a depth and zeal she hadn't thought possible.

As if he could hear the thoughts swirling in her mind, Joshua slipped his finger under her chin and lifted until she met his stare.

"How did you know something was amiss?" she asked.

"Burns brought a copy of the duke's last will and testament. You were to inherit a larger sum than you expected, and it would multiply greatly if Pierce did not make amends with you." He kissed her chastely, giving Kate time to think through what he'd said. His lips only proved distracting, so she pulled away.

"Why would that lead you to think I was in danger?" she asked.

"It also stated that if you were to perish before you reconciled with your father, he would receive his full inheritance with no stipulations." Joshua brushed her cheek, trailing his finger down her throat and lightly over the cut on her neck. "I deduced quickly he'd been the one to set the fire."

"I have always admired your deductive reasoning skills," she laughed.

"Truly?" He glared at her with suspicion. "You've never uttered a word of it to me before."

"I am saying it now," Kate countered.

Her mother cleared her throat. "What of you, my lord? What do you admire about *my daughter*?"

The possessiveness in her mother's tone had Kate grinning. She much liked these two, people she loved greatly, feeling such fierce protectiveness toward her.

"And do not waste your words on me," A'laya huffed. She pushed to her feet and made her way to the back office, giving Joshua and Kate a moment of privacy before the magistrate arrived.

"You needn't let her push you into—" Kate attempted to brush off her mother's question.

She did not seek to force Joshua into speaking more of his feelings if he weren't prepared to do so.

Yet, her mind kept going over his words—*I love her with complete abandon*.

Besides the love blossoming between mother and daughter, Kate had never been loved with anything even close to recklessness—complete or otherwise. She'd always been held at arm's length—by her parents, by her father's congregation, and by those she'd considered friends.

The notion that she was loved so now did not make sense in her mind.

"Kate?" Without her noticing, Joshua had stood and knelt before her, taking her hands in his. His warmth banished the cold numbness that'd overtaken them. "I meant what I said earlier. I love you with a force so insistent I find an hour without you is simply not acceptable. I understand your concerns, with your home and everything with your mother. However, I will be here for you through it all, in whatever capacity you allow. Even if you only desire a friend."

She stood, pulling Joshua to his feet with her. "Then I think you should know"—she paused, drawing in a deep breath as his shoulders tightened with tension—"I meant every word I said, too. I love you, Joshua, I have for a very long time, though I could not see it clearly because I was uncertain what love looked like between two people. I want you, all of you, and for far more than a friend. I cannot be myself unless I'm with you. Here in Cheapside or at your townhouse... anywhere, as long as I am with you."

There was nothing else to say. She loved him, and he loved her.

Kate's chest burst with the potential of her future—*their* future. It had only taken opening herself to the possibilities that fate had aligned for her.

Perhaps fortune's final folly had been bringing Joshua into her life.

But it would be Kate who had the last laugh. And she did—laugh—but only for a brief moment before Joshua swept her into his arms, twirling her about the room until they were both laughing.

"I loved you as simply Miss Kate Elliott." He set his forehead against hers as he halted, his stare turning serious. "I will love you even if you wish to be addressed as Lady Katherina De Vere. Though I find I think I would love you most if you agreed to be Lady Stuart, my wife."

A completely overwhelming happiness filled Kate so quickly, it nearly brought tears to her eyes once more.

"As long as we are together, Joshua, I can be Miss Kate or Lady Katherina," Kate said with a smile so wide, she knew she could not hide her joy. "I find I much enjoy the sound of Lady Stuart, as well."

EPILOGUE

KATE FELL INTO her favorite chair before the fire in Joshua's study at their Cavendish Square townhouse, exhausted from her day at the schoolroom. The last of the new furniture had arrived that morning, as well as two dozen heavy boxes with new primers and books for her students. The schoolroom would reopen and resume class as normal the following week.

And it was all due to Joshua.

Speaking of her soon-to-be husband, he currently sat behind his desk, writing furiously.

He worked so intently he hadn't noticed Kate enter the room or close the door or all but crash into her chair.

"Is everything as it should be?" she asked, hesitant to interrupt him.

At the sound of her voice, Joshua set down his quill, dusted the paper to dry the ink, and crossed the room to her.

"Welcome home, my love." He lowered himself into the chair next to her, and she immediately wiggled onto his lap. Truthfully, the chair wasn't overly comfortable, but it was large enough for both of them. "I missed you dreadfully. How was your day?"

Over the course of the last three months, Kate had come to think of Joshua's townhouse as her home, as well. She loved everything about the house, especially how welcome everyone made her feel—from the servants, all the way to Dolly.

They loved and accepted her without reservations.

It had become their way of handling everything that stood in their path.

They faced all things with complete abandon.

Their love for one another.

Their journey to restore the schoolroom.

The trial against her father, the Earl of Holderness.

And, more recently, their quest to find the marriage log from her mother's family's vicarage.

"My day was splendid," she purred, fitting her body against his. "Everything is ready for my students. What of yours? You appeared awfully distracted when I came in."

Joshua sighed. Since the Lord High Steward had chosen to pursue charges against her father, the earl's barrister had brought into question not his client's guilt or innocence, but Kate's right to inherit the Shrewbury estate. The last month, with Mr. Burns' assistance following his fallout with, and his utter distaste for his previous client, they'd written tirelessly, trying to locate any documentation of her mother's marriage to

De Vere. The servants from Shrewbury had gladly testified to the facts as they knew them, but more was needed. Joshua and Burns wanted to prove Kate's right to her inheritance, and with Walter's letter, his will, and the vicarage log, everything would work in her favor.

"Burns thinks the log resides at Shrewbury Gardens, taken by the duchess after you and your mother were cast out."

"It could be anywhere," Kate said.

He tapped the tip of her nose before kissing her gently. "Yes. But we will not give up."

"Search with complete abandon?"

The door to the study flew open, and Dolly bustled in, Kate's mother not far behind. The pair had quickly taken to one another since A'laya had agreed to live in Cavendish Square with Kate, and were as close as Dolly had been with Joshua's grandmother.

"The *Post*, it has arrived." Dolly waved the afternoon paper high above her head. "I cannot believe it, my dear A'laya. It finally happened."

Kate slid off Joshua's lap and snatched the *Post* as the two women sat on the lounge.

"Page two," her mother called, pointing at the paper. "Open it to the second page. Top corner. You cannot miss it."

Kate scanned the paper.

Joshua's breath warmed her neck as he looked on over her shoulder.

Finally, she found what she was looking for…

It is with great honor that Lord Joshua Stuart, son of the Duke and Duchess of Beaufort, hereby maketh known his intentions to wed Lady Katherina De Vere, granddaughter of the Right Honorable Lord and Lady Oderton, and daughter of the Right

Honorable Countess of Holderness.

Kate smiled at the honor paid to her mother's parents and continued reading as it went on to list the date of their upcoming nuptials.

Only a few short weeks away. Soon, she would be Lady Stuart and could do away with the remnants of the family who'd torn her and her mother apart. While Kate had accepted her place as a lady, her mother still refused the title, going simply by *A'laya* to anyone she met. Her mother had taken to teaching alongside Kate and helping her arrange the schoolroom.

Their relationship had become as natural as any between a mother and daughter.

They laughed often. They cried just as frequently.

But they loved one another at all times.

And this had come to include Joshua and Dolly, as well.

"I love you." The announcement was perfect—simple, as she'd requested. "Thank you for bringing me home."

If she spoke of the night of the fire or the gradual progression after, Kate was uncertain. Truly, she was simply thanking him for everything he'd done for her. Especially helping her discover who she was and who she was fated to be by his side.

"Dinner is waiting," Dolly announced with a clap of her hands. "A'laya has taught Cook one of her family dishes. I do not wish to spoil the surprise; however, it will melt if we do not hurry."

Joshua leapt to his feet and held his hand out for Kate. "My love?"

Placing her hand in his, she stood, rising to

her tiptoes to press her lips to his. "We shan't want to ruin a lovely dish."

As they departed the study, Joshua slowed his pace until Kate's mother and Dolly were several feet ahead of them before he leaned down and murmured in her ear, "Thank you for making this my home again."

AUTHOR'S NOTES

Thank you for reading *Fortune's Final Folly!* If
you enjoyed *Fortune's Final Folly*, be sure to write
a brief review at any retailer.

I'd love to hear from you!
You can contact me at:
Christina@christinamcknight.com
Or write me at:
P.O. Box 1017
Patterson, CA 95363

www.ChristinaMcKnight.com
Check out my website for giveaways, book
reviews, and information on my upcoming
projects, or connect with me through social
media at:
Twitter: @CMcKnightWriter
Facebook:
www.facebook.com/christinamcknightwriter
Goodreads:
www.goodreads.com/ChristinaMcKnight

Sign up for my newsletter here:
http://hyperurl.co/CMNL

Turn the page for an excerpt from
Fated for the Duke,
where love and magic collide at the
racetrack

AN EXCERPT FROM
FATED FOR THE DUKE

Sunderland, England
December 1802

EMILIA, ALONG WITH her three siblings and their *seanmhair*, lowered themselves into the root cellar, taking the long ladder down one rung at a time, their grandmother bringing up the rear. The pungent, heavy aroma of ripening vegetables and her father's treasured wine barrels greeted Emilia much like a warm, familiar embrace.

Each year, for all her life, it had been the same.

Seanmhair Ailis had brought Emilia, Moire, Iain, and Catriona into the musty cellar every year since their births. As they each learned to walk without assistance, the first ladder they had descended led into this dark, dank, windowless room through a trap door in their butler's pantry. And *Seanmhair* demanded they each make the climb unassisted and without a candle to guide them.

It had been a frightening experience when Emilia was younger, but as her siblings were born, and she was charged with minding them, the practice became one of routine and comfort as they lost sight of the importance of the journey. Her mother and father no longer participated and were known to chastise *Seanmhair* for her old-world traditions.

"Come now, me wee ones," *Seanmhair* said, gathering Emilia and her siblings close as she knelt down to look each in the eyes, her knees cracking with the effort. "Do ye ken why we be down here?"

Emilia remained silent, the thick air in the room dampening her short locks as if she stood not in a root cellar, but in a light spring mist.

It was not her place to answer *Seanmhair* Ailis. She'd made the climb down into the root cellar for ten years now. No, on this day, it was Moire, Emilia's youngest sister—aged only five winters—who was to speak.

Seanmhair's crystal blue stare fairly glowed in the dark, cramped space as she took in each child in turn. Though her glare was intense, Emilia saw the faint, green glow hovering about the old woman. Even with *Seanmhair* Ailis's aged and weathered appearance, her drooping cheeks and the creases about her eyes and mouth, Emilia saw it.

Love.

Seanmhair Ailis loved them all very much.

It made this moment all the more imperative. Ailis wasn't attempting to frighten them or cause them any lasting night terrors. No, she was warning them...*preparing* them for a future they may not escape as she had.

Catriona sighed, elbowing Moire to get on with answering the question.

Moire, named for one of their Scottish ancestors, straightened her shoulders and notched up her chin a degree as she mirrored *Seanmhair's* serious glare and recited what she'd been made to memorize. "We mustn't ever put from mind that we are all special. Our gifts, blessed unto us by our Dalais ancestors, are of great privilege and should not be used for evil. We are descendants of a trio of powerful siblings—Niall, Sorcha, and Caitriona—who gave up their lives to bring each of us into this world." Moire picked at the fraying edge of her pinafore, and Emilia had the nearly overpowering urge to assist her, to speak up and tell their grandmother what she waited to hear.

When Emilia made to do just that, *Seanmhair's* piercing blue eyes swung her way—a warning to remain silent.

As swiftly as the warning glare had turned to Emilia, the elder woman turned back to Moire with an encouraging nod. "Go on, *m'eudail*."

Moire's lips pulled wide in a smile that had enchanted their entire family since the girl's birth. Emilia's sister loved when their grandmother spoke to them in her native Scottish tongue and called her things like *my darling*. "We are to trust in our gifts. We are to trust in one another. And, above all else, we are to be leery of any person not of Dalais blood."

"Very good, me sweet." Their *seanmhair* pushed to her feet, though even at full height she was little taller than Emilia and Iain. If not for her ailing, stooped body and grey hair, she could easily pass for a child from a distance. Though, up close, her dress, her speech, and her repose were of a different time. "Now, tell me, me bairns, what know ye of this moment?"

Iain grunted and crossed his arms. "I despise this part."

"What have I told ye, lad?" *Seanmhair* snapped, placing her crooked, knotty hand on Iain's shoulder.

Emilia's brother stared at his scuffed boots as he transferred his weight from one foot to the other. "That the gifts chose us, and there is naught we can say about it. But it still isn't fair, not one little bit that Em, Moire, and Cat were chosen, and I am nothing…barely a Noble at all."

"Me darling lad." Their grandmother's tone softened, and she stepped until she faced Iain, her fingers lifting his chin until he stared directly at her. "Ye were blessed with beauty, wealth, and title. The luck born of a male heir. Ye canna expect to have everything."

Iain pulled away from his *seanmhair*. "I'd rather have the mark and a gift like my great-great-great-great-grandfather, Lochlan."

"You know males of the Dalais bloodline have not been blessed with the mark for many decades," Cat chimed in. "Even Father was given no gift, and he is strong, and brave, and courageous."

"And a bore," Iain mumbled.

Moire giggled at her brother's proclamation.

Even Emilia could not suppress a grin,

though she did not dare laugh at such a solemn time.

"Moire," the older woman prodded, giving the girl's long, fiery red plait a gentle tug. "What do ye see?"

The girl gulped, her shoulders quaking ever so slightly. "I'd rather Cat or Em speak first."

"Verra well." *Seanmhair* turned to Emilia, the first grandchild born with the legacy mark on her left hip. A simple triangle, but a gift their family feared would not be bestowed upon the Noble family again. "What do ye see, me wee lass?"

It hadn't been until Emilia began to speak that her family had discovered her special gift. She could see the energy of those around her with the enhanced ability to recognize when another was lying. With her grandmother's help, Emilia had worked to understand what each color and hazy glow meant.

"I see…" Her words trailed off as a dark, brownish-yellow surrounded the woman. Her *seanmhair* was fatigued, yet other colors pushed through as Emilia scrutinized her grandmother. "Violet and gold show you are imparting great wisdom. And green, as always, envelops you."

Love. Kindness. Caring.

Seanmhair Ailis nodded curtly and turned to Cat. "And ye, me wee kitten?"

Cat closed her eyes, her brow pulling low with her effort. Catriona had been the most impacted by her gift: the ability to connect with another's emotional state. With great work, their grandmother had taught Cat how to harness her gift and not allow it to overwhelm her. For a period, Cat had been utterly weighed down by the burdens of those around her, whether it be someone in their family or even the villagers they passed in town.

Emilia watched as Cat worried her bottom lip until a tiny bead of blood marred her perfect flesh.

If Emilia had been given a choice, she would have taken all three gifts unto herself, if only to save her two sisters from the oppressive nature of their abilities.

The gift of sight. The gift of empathy. And the gift to read another's energy force.

Seanmhair Ailis had been the only one of her siblings chosen, though she'd been given thrice the gifts, and the completed legacy mark: three overlaid triangles. If one combined Emilia's, Cat's, and Moire's marks, it would mirror the birthmark on their grandmother's chest, just below her collarbone.

"I see you are frantic, *Seanmhair*. There is an urgency surrounding you I do not understand." Cat glanced at Moire, begging her to help, but her younger sister averted her gaze.

"Moire?" Emilia questioned.

"*Seanmhair* is not long for this world," Moire whispered before a cry escaped her. "*Seanmhair* Ailis, I wish to go back above. I do not want to do this any longer. My vision…it is cruel, and I will not allow it to come true."

"Tsk-tsk." Their grandmother shook her head but not in sorrow. "Me dearest, Moire. Ye may see the future, but ye can do naught to change it. It not be the way of things. Not at all."

Iain pushed back into the circle Emilia, Moire, Cat, and their *seanmhair* had created without them realizing it.

"Tell us Moire is wrong," Iain demanded. "She is but a baby and cannot know what she says." He looked to his eldest sister for something—perhaps guidance—and Emilia longed to reassure him of their future. Alas, she could not.

Despite their shared eye color and appearances, it was Emilia who had hair of the palest blond, nearly white in the sun, which set her apart from her siblings and even her *seanmhair*.

At eight, Emilia's younger brother, Iain, was a boy surrounded by strong women, their Scottish heritage, pale skin, and fiery hair only making their spirit more apparent. While he shared the family's coloring as well as their piercing blue eyes, he was more like their father—a boy willing to allow the women in his family to lead.

Perhaps the boy had more spirit then they'd given him credit for.

Iain turned to Emilia, looking for an ally. "Em, tell them this is absurd. *Seanmhair* is well and will be going nowhere. Not for a long, long time. We need her. You have yet to master your gift, and Moire…can we trust her visions?"

Emilia knew Moire spoke only the truth. Sometimes, her gift was also a curse, just as it was for Catriona and Moire.

"Moire be correct, wee ones." *Seanmhair* pulled all four children close, and Emilia accepted her embrace, pushing farther into her hold as if them all banding together and never letting go could stop her grandmother's encroaching fate. "I be gone soon enough, and the group of ye shall move on from Dalais Forge—Edinburgh, Bath, and London. The world is yours to explore. But ye must stay close. Depend on each other. Listen to one another."

"Yes, *Seanmhair* Ailis," they spoke in unison, each bowing their heads.

Emilia's chest ached at the thought of living even a moment without her grandmother near.

She wanted to cry, to wail about the unfairness of it all, to stomp her foot and demand it not come to pass.

Alas, her bout of anger and sadness would do naught to change their future.

"Now, me wee lasses, remember…one day a friend, and the next a foe. Ye need to rely on each other, trust in only each other. I won't be here to protect ye much longer."

"What of me?" Iain demanded, his tone rising in panic.

"Ye, lad, will listen to ye sisters." Her stern words had Iain swallowing any retort he may have had. "These three care for ye, Iain. Even when ye think ye know best, ye don't."

Emilia thought her *seanmhair* was being too harsh and severe with Iain.

But, again, she kept quiet.

"It is getting late, and me bones are aching." *Seanmhair* Ailis swept her long, grey hair back over her shoulder and fixed each of them with one last stare. "Ye all need to find ye beds. Off with the lot of ye."

Iain was the first to turn and scurry up the ladder into the butler's pantry. His footsteps could be heard above as he fled. Cat was far more hesitant in her departure, her steps slow as she climbed into the light from above and waited for her sisters to follow. Finally, Emilia took hold of the lower rung and hoisted herself up as her *seanmhair* spoke in a hushed voice to Moire. Her words of caution drifted up to Emilia…

"Moire, me wee darling, ye canna speak of that to ye sister. The future be what it is, with or without ye meddling…"

Emilia climbed ever higher until she reached the top, Catriona's soft cries falling from above, even though her *seanmhair's* words tempted

Emilia back down to the cellar. Despite her tears, Cat held her hand out to help Emilia out.

Behind them, they listened to the scraping of Moire's half-boots as she too climbed up the ladder. The day seemed final: the end of a long-held, sacred tradition.

Emilia did not want to move away from Dalais Forge, nor be without her *seanmhair*.

Available now in e-book, paperback, and audiobook

ABOUT THE AUTHOR

USA TODAY Bestselling Author Christina McKnight writes emotional and intricate Regency Romance with strong women and maverick heroes.

Her books combine romance and mystery, exploring themes of redemption and forgiveness. When she's not writing, Christina enjoys trying new coffeehouses, visiting wine bars, traveling the world, and watching television.

Email: Christina@ChristinaMcKnight.com
Follow her on Twitter: @CMcKnightWriter
Keep up to date on her releases:
www.christinamcknight.com
Like Christina's FB Author page:
ChristinaMcKnightWriter
Sign up for Christina's newsletter:
http://hyperurl.co/CMNL